I0456769

A SPELL TO DISCOVER

THE WITCH OF HENBANE ISLAND

POPPY BRIDGEMAN

Ebook ISBN: 978-1-990509-53-7
Paperback ISBN: 978-1-990509-54-4
Audio book ISBN:978-1-990509-55-1

Copyright © 2025by P A Wilson

All rights reserved.

No part of this book may be reproduced in any form or by any electronic or mechanical means, including information storage and retrieval systems, without written permission from the author, except for the use of brief quotations in a book review.

Cover created by Getcovers

FREE BOOK

Claim your copy of Magic Will Out when you sign up for my newsletter and follow Cossi as she seeks answers to her past.

1

I was blown away by how different Henbane felt now that the festival was underway. I stood in my booth, looking out over the crowd. There were visitors, sure, but I had no idea this many people lived on Henbane. How had I missed what must be more than half the population?

I knew this wasn't the kind of place where people commuted to work Monday through Friday, but surely I would have seen some of these witches around. And here we were on Friday, the first day of the festival, and I had no clue who was a visitor and who was a resident I'd simply never met.

The main thing I felt in my core was that I belonged with these witches and shifters, and I would do anything to protect my new life here.

"These are pretty," a woman said as she handled one of the talisman blanks I was giving out.

The idea had come to me after I learned more about the fifteen that arrived in a box. Those ones were wrong somehow, but the concept of having a piece of jewelry that could double as protection, or a power bank appealed to me. I didn't have a lot of time to put the booth together—more of a counter with supports and fabric walls than an actual structure—so I was grateful for any inspiration.

"I can burn a symbol into it if you like," I said.

She looked at me, and her emotions were a bit... spinny was the only word that seemed to fit. I read interest, but the color was closer to worry, and the aroma of citrus fruits usually meant curiosity.

"I heard about you," she said. "My name is Bud. Buddleia Twotrees, to be exact."

So, off-island—otherwise she'd have done more than just hear about me. "Where do you live? I had no idea there were any witches around until I came here."

"Kincolith. It's way up north. Yes, you grew up thinking you were a plain, right?"

"Plain? Is that what humans without magic are called?" I'd been calling them normal or mundane, and no one had corrected me. I didn't like using normal—it kind of implied that my new family wasn't. I liked plain because it felt more honest. We're all human, just some of us have a little extra. Like the difference between vanilla and French vanilla ice cream.

"Plain, simple, mortal—there are lots of expressions. I'd like a fir tree, please."

I picked up the wood-burning pen I kept under the counter and traced out an image that looked a bit like a child's Christmas tree drawing. It turned out okay. I wouldn't be winning any art awards, but anyone could decipher the image—unlike the fifteen in my apartment that kept shifting into something new all the time.

I blew on the wood to cool it. "Here you go. All ready for you to imbue with whatever magic you want."

"Oh, so really a blank. That's useful," Bud said, then

dropped the disk into her pocket. Each one had a small hole so it could be strung on a cord or chain. "I'll take one of these flyers. Maybe I'll be back."

The flyers were spread out on the counter—two for the Inner Spell, one explaining the B&B and the other the retreat. Then there were catalogs to order teas and potions from Mr. Macy, a few gardening tip sheets from Valerie in the Earth Witch village, and a contact sheet for Raziel's Books, where I lived. Phillip owned the store and had been my mentor when I first arrived.

"I hear you're giving out blanks," Jeffrey Peak said. "Where did you get the wood?"

Jeffrey had regained his health after being the victim of a memory disruption spell and days held captive by a killer. He still looked every inch the retired biker I'd met in my first few days on the island. His memory was still spotty, but it was coming back in bits every day.

"Destroyer found me a fallen oak branch," I said. Destroyer was my familiar, a crow with delusions of grandeur and empire—maybe not so much delusions. "There's no magic. Lance showed me how to make the discs. They've been quite popular."

"I imagine. Most of us had them as kids, but I like the idea of bringing them back. Can I see one?"

I pushed the tray of various-sized blanks toward him. "Why don't you take one?"

He pushed his finger through the small pile but didn't select any. He paused, then nodded. "No magic. Have you thought of putting a light protection spell on them?"

I didn't have enough confidence in my power to cast that many spells. "I thought every witch who took one would want only their own magic involved."

He looked at the tray again and made a satisfied noise.

"You're right. Well, I must be off. We solitaries are sharing a booth, and it's my shift. Have a successful day."

Then he was gone, leaving me to wonder why he'd felt the need to test the objects. I tried to ignore the little voice inside that said you made a mistake and believe it was just curiosity on his part.

The aroma of grilled meat drifted over from a few booths away. Sheena was serving lunch. I glanced over—no line yet, and nothing in my booth needed constant attention. It was the perfect time to grab one of her burgers.

Before I could step away, D arrived with two burgers and two pints of beer.

"I got you covered," he said, placing a glass and a plate on the counter. "How are you liking your first festival?"

"I love it." I took a bite and focused on the burst of flavor on my tongue for a moment before swallowing. "I can't believe this is going to last five days. Aren't people going to get tired of it?"

"Nope. Every day has a different focus. On the last day, it's mostly final purchases and packing, but the day before that is the big party. It might be different next year, but don't forget—we haven't had a place for people without friends or family to visit. The mainland communities can't host their own festivals. No way to keep it hidden."

Concealing the paranormals—that was the topic of the discussion being held in the business center on Main Street. A group of Henbane residents and one mainland witch were trying to find a way to keep the paranormal world safe from the plain human one.

2

_____

left, and I talked to more people until the festival slowed down. By then, most of my talisman blanks were gone, and I'd planned for them to last the whole festival. So good news and bad news, I guess.

I didn't have time to make more, but my mind automatically started reviewing my packed schedule. Not that many items on it—the festival and lessons with Mrs. Vestum. I was supposed to go to her when the day closed out. Then bed. I was thankful The Inner Spell was fully booked; otherwise, I'd have moved out there and be faced with a bike ride after lessons. I'm not exactly complaining, but I keep thinking my days and nights would slow down, and something always comes along to pile more on. I'm not sure where my breaking point is, but I expect it isn't too far away.

The minute I stopped listing what was on my shoulders, my marketing lessons kicked in. This was a limited market. I could manage my dwindling supply by promising locals I would make and deliver more later. Two birds, one stone. I would get to know a lot more of my fellow Henbanians— that didn't sound right.

"Why are you killing birds with stones?" Destroyer, my familiar, asked in my mind.

I hated that he could hear my thoughts but had to admit it came in handy more than once. "It's just an expression about efficiency."

"And killing birds."

I guess I hadn't thought about it that way when I didn't chat with animals on a regular basis. And if I was actually speaking, I might have caught myself. "I didn't mean to offend. I promise to think before I think."

"I'm the only one who hears you. But I am feeling magnanimous, so you are pardoned. Just don't talk about swinging or skinning cats. Non-witches have very violent ways of speaking."

"I suppose they do. Now go back to sleep."

"Phillip is coming to see you." Destroyer broke off communication, which was a good thing, because I hadn't mastered the art of carrying on a conversation in my head while talking to someone in front of me.

A few minutes later, Phillip joined me at the counter, his gaze immediately going to the bowl of talisman blanks.

"I've heard good things about your booth, Cossi," he said. His recent injuries still showed on his hand, where he claimed he'd banged it against a bookshelf. He hadn't recovered all his color yet, but the bug he'd caught last week was definitely over. He didn't look like he was about to curl up in a corner and sleep for a week, for a change.

"Thanks for letting me know," I said. "I can do more next year, but it's good to know my lack of knowledge hasn't hurt me."

He nodded, as if I'd said the right thing. As a mentor, he was more of a business coach. I mean, I could probably run the bookstore on my own. But his magical teaching wasn't just lacking—it was nonexistent. Since Mrs. V took over as my mentor, I'd come to understand exactly what it took to make the move from totally unaware of the paranormal world to full-fledged witch.

"One of the witches from Nanaimo asked if you were selling any books for me, because you had other witches' products in your booth." He scanned my counter as he spoke.

"Do you want to sell some here?" I had a bit of room, and I was sure it would be easy to load some actual inventory into my payment app. "I'll make room, but you probably don't want to leave them out overnight."

"No, the dampness would affect the paper. I can create a list of my most popular books for you, much like Peter Macy and Valerie Nightshade have with their products." He lifted his gaze from the bowl and looked right into my eyes. It was a little disconcerting, like he was reading into my deepest thoughts. "That might be a good use for your presence in future years. This could be a hub for information. Since you've successfully found a way to bring more strangers here, perhaps it should be your responsibility to ensure they are kept out of trouble."

I wasn't going to answer that. Not in a crowded venue, or in our shared kitchen. The council had approved my change of business to include a B&B, and I was really surprised that their emotions had been all positive. I was not going to become the tour guide for Henbane. Mostly because I didn't want to, and because exploring seemed to be on the must-do list for the new visitors.

"Did you bring a list? Of the books?" I asked to get us back on a safer topic.

"I'll make one up. I'm glad you are successful, Cossi. Your parents would be proud."

He walked away before I could thank him. Although his tone had been odd, like he was disappointed despite the words he chose. I couldn't read his emotions in any way. Mrs. V had offered me some tea to blunt my powers. Every witch and shifter on Henbane whose power had any element of reading people drank it. The tea blunted the powers enough to function. Imagine the onslaught of emotions I'd face if I was at full function. I still didn't like feeling the loss—like a phantom limb. At least I would get it back in a couple of days.

A group of shifters gathered in the walkway in front of my booth, not blocking traffic, but setting up fiddles and a harp. In moments, they were entertaining the crowd with tunes that felt like old Irish airs but were dragged from the top pop music lists.

"Ah, there you are," Ms. Flor said as she rushed up to my booth. "Our committee has finished for the day, so I'll have a chance to enjoy the festival. Before you ask, we spent most of the time introducing ourselves and sharing stories, so nothing to report—even if we hadn't agreed to keep everything under wraps."

"I'm glad you have time to meet people and have some fun," I said, not sure what else I was supposed to contribute. Ms. Flor was always breathless, as though she had to run through life to get everything done.

"That's what I wanted to ask. Your other guests and I want to have a small party. Up at The Inner Spell. Celebrate our status as your first guests. I don't know how to arrange for food and drink. Can you tell me who to ask?"

Despite her constant assurances that I didn't need to take care of the people staying up at the chalets, I felt guilty about what I thought of as abandoning them. Tonight I wasn't even planning to check in on them. A celebratory party sounded fun, but Mrs. V already had a full slate of magic work for me tonight.

"I can ask Jan," I said, pulling out my phone. "He's preparing for tomorrow, so I'm sure he has what you need." The food vendors changed every day of the festival so that residents who didn't want to attend had somewhere to eat. Today, Sheena. Tomorrow, Jan. The next day, Zoe from Food For Us.

"Just give me his contact information," she said. "I can talk to him while I wander around. And don't look so guilty. We are all quite capable of managing, and I'll ensure we keep the damage to a minimum."

I laughed and hoped she was kidding about the damage. "Ms. Flor, I can't ask people to pay me for accommodation and then not do my job." I read off Jan's number after voicing my objections.

"Call me Zinnia. I know we'll be great friends. Since I'll be staying around, we can discuss a discount rate for my rooms later. In exchange for my services?" She gave a little laugh.

It seemed like a good compromise. I watched her weave her way through the crowds. We would be friends; I could tell, even without my powers. In my new life, people of all ages became close. I sent a text to Jan telling him she'd be in touch and to charge the bill to me.

3

———

By the time the festival activities started to wind down for the day, I was looking forward to a shower and a bit of quiet. Instead, I was headed to Mrs. V's for lessons, so I'd have to settle for a change of clothes. No one else seemed to be feeling the effects of standing in a booth all day, so there was probably a spell I didn't know about. I know it's my responsibility to ask about magical stuff, but there is such a huge gap in my knowledge, I didn't know when I should ask a question. Every time I thought to ask, either there was no one around or something more important came up.

I made a mental note to ask Mrs. V when I got to her place. I still had an hour before the horn blew to signal the end of the festival day. The attendees would then head off to dinner, or parties, or simply to bed. I'd release the ties that held the curtain back during the day. The front of the booth would then be covered, and the whole area would look like some kind of Ren Faire arena. A quick spell to protect from any rain or other weather and I'd be done.

My last visitor left, and it looked like I wouldn't attract

much more attention. Unlike the vendors, the participants could leave before the horn, and more of them headed for the streets and paths leading into the other areas of Henbane every time I peeked out.

"Doc Rene has been unusually busy this year." The words came from the side of my tent. A woman's voice, but not one I recognized.

I didn't have much choice in listening in—I guess I could have tried to focus on something else, but they were talking in the open, more or less, and I didn't have any customers. And to be frank, I was bored enough to crave a little distraction.

"Yes, but it's all these new people," a man said. "They don't know how to take care of themselves. They keep going like it's their only chance to experience the festival."

"Maybe they're right," the woman said with a sigh—of regret? Frustration? I was so used to reading emotions, I felt cut off from the world. "If anything goes wrong, the council might refuse to allow visitors."

That would be a bad decision. I wasn't just thinking about my business—interacting with the mainland witches and shifters kept us informed of the realities. The committee would never find a solution to the problems paranormals living in cities experience without meeting in person. I reached my hand out to pull aside the side curtain to see who was doing the talking.

"That's not going to happen," the man said. "We need visitors these days. And other communities like Henbane exist out there."

I pulled my hand back. What? Of course this wasn't the only hidden island of paranormals. Why did I assume we were the only one? A thousand other questions ripped through my mind.

"What's happening?" Destroyer snapped at me, pulling my thoughts back from the edge of sanity.

"Nothing. I just learned something exciting." I fully expected him to say I got excited about everything, but he just cawed a grumble and retreated from my head.

The two witches hadn't left while I spoke to my familiar, and I caught the tail end of a statement by the woman: "... sick tent filled up."

This time, I pulled the drape aside. If people were getting sick, I needed more details. My talisman blanks had gained attention, and both Phillip and Buddleia Twotrees had made a point of mentioning them. Did people think my giveaways were causing illness?

The two witches glanced my way when I peeked out. I didn't know their names, but I'd seen them a few times in the Earth Witch village, so they weren't visitors.

"Sorry. Were we disturbing you?" the woman asked. "We're just catching a breather in the shade before we head home."

"It must be roasting out there," I said, acknowledging the heatwave that arrived with the festival. "I couldn't help overhearing you say people are falling ill."

The man looked concerned—not by me eavesdropping, I hoped. "The mainlanders don't take care of themselves. It seems odd that they don't know to drink enough water when everyone can see it's needed."

So, probably nothing to do with me. My stupid inner self didn't believe it, but I told her to shut up. "Is Doc Rene coping? If there are too many, maybe I can help out."

The woman shook her head and smiled, giving her companion a poke. "She's fine. Lilibeth is with her. Herman is exaggerating. I don't think we've met. I'm Izzie Darkberry and this is Herman Busch."

"You've both just returned to Henbane, right? I'm Cossi Fortuna. Good to meet you."

"We know who you are, dear," Herman said. "Welcome to your real life. And Izzie is right; I tend to get a bit dramatic sometimes. The opera in me busting out, if you will."

"Like he said, mostly it's the people visiting," Izzie said.

"I think they're really excited about being here," I said, trying to calm that little voice inside more than anything. "There's no festival outside the hidden communities, so they forget to take care of themselves."

"Probably," Herman said. "It's just... well, of course we've only got secondhand information, but with all the recent murders it does make one wonder."

Izzie poked him again, this time harder and accompanied it with a tsk. "See what I mean? Drama. I'll pop by tomorrow to see what you've got in your booth. Maybe book one of your chalets for a little romantic dinner?"

She led Herman away before I had a chance to say the chalets were pretty far from romantic.

4

I cast the spell of protection over my booth and headed home. Beulah, my bike, waited for me in the corral just off to the side of the clearing. A two-minute ride to my apartment over the bookstore. Sure, I could have walked, but I needed every minute I could squeeze out between closing the booth and arriving at Mrs. V's.

I saw Phillip through the window as I rode by, talking to a witch who seemed to have shriveled into his clothes. Even older than Zoe and Mrs. V. A reminder that Henbane was a relatively new community, and that on the mainland, paranormal humans had been around since the beginning. The customer looked like he could remember the origins of civilization.

Upstairs, I jumped in the shower and washed my hair. It would just have to dry in a frizz. I'd deal with taming it tomorrow. A fresh set of clothes, including a lilac tee and peasant skirt, left me feeling ready to take on whatever faced me in the way of lessons. My stomach rumbled now that the aches had gone from my body. Mrs. V might not have food, and even if she did, it tended to be cheese or peanut butter sandwiches.

I called Jan and placed a takeout order. Two bowls of vegetable stew and a side of fries for us to share.

I pulled my hair into a bun in an effort to keep it from blooming into a giant red puffball and left.

THE DOOR WAS open as usual. I called out as I stepped inside my mentor's house. "I brought dinner."

"Come on back," Mrs. V answered.

She wasn't in the kitchen when I got there. Mrs. V had a secret room for storing all her magical artifacts, and I guessed that's where she was. Tulip meow-growled from that direction, confirming my guess.

I put the meals on the counter, stole a fry to prove to my stomach that I hadn't forgotten it, and reached for the spoons and china bowls. No eating out of paper for us.

"Come eat while it's hot," I called.

She stepped in and nodded at the table setting. "Put a little in a saucer for Tulip and cool it, please."

As grouchy and demanding as she was to humans, Mrs. V seemed to have a mushy spot for animals. She pretended to be annoyed by Destroyer, but always had water and a bowl of seeds on hand.

"Eat first," I said. "Standing all day builds up a surprising appetite."

She sat and took a spoonful of her stew, placing a fry on top before eating. "Jan is a good cook," she muttered after swallowing. "We're lucky to have him."

Wow. A compliment for someone?

We ate in relative silence—Tulip's slurping and growl-purring wasn't conversation even for me.

"She growls a lot," I said as I cleared the dishes. "Are you sure she's going to be tame enough?"

"Is your crow tame?" Mrs. V snapped. I guess I'd offended her somehow.

"He's building an animal empire and army. So, I guess more civilized than tamed."

"Crows were civilized when humans were hiding in caves," he said in my mind.

I passed it on, with the caveat that I had no idea how long ago crows existed.

She laughed, and I almost dropped the bowl I was washing. There was definitely something going on. She'd never done much more than smile before.

I placed my spell journal on the table after filling water glasses. "What are we working on tonight?"

"I want you to cast a protection spell on yourself," she said. "Then we will start the investigation into all the pieces we have that may lead to finding our puppet master."

Wow. I kind of thought we'd leave all that until the festival was over and the visitors had left us. "Is my spell-casting affected by the tea to mute my emotions?" I'd been told it faded during the day, and I'd need to refresh the muffle one in the morning.

"Did you cast the spell on your booth?" she asked, without any attitude of you've done something wrong.

"Yes, of course," I said.

"And did you feel any unusual effects?" Again, no subtle dig at my abilities.

"No. So I guess the answer is no?"

She gave me the side-eye. So she was still capable of making me feel in the wrong for no reason.

I closed my eyes and let go of my disappointment. When I opened them again, I made a sigil and said the spell—no need for ingredients on this one. In fact, most of the balms, smokes, and oils I'd been using in the past were training techniques. I rarely needed the help now.

Mrs. V put the journal on the table. "We want to remove the spell holding the book closed. Nothing else until we see inside. What do you suggest?"

I brushed my fingers over the leather. There was magic, but it was faint. "When we searched his room, Mark did a spell to muffle my magic. I was able to get through the barrier Martin placed, but only for about twenty minutes. And I wasn't expelled—it just made me increasingly uncomfortable."

"That tells us Martin is unlikely to have used a violent spell on the journal. If we get it wrong, there won't be an explosion."

Would Martin want someone to read the book if he died? It had been taped behind the drawer of the nightstand in his room. We only searched because we were investigating his murder. "He didn't want someone to stumble on the book and read what was inside. That means it contains a secret."

"Yes, one we hope will lead us to the witch behind all the killings."

Only Phillip and I lived in the apartment. Was it meant to stop us? None of my thoughts were leading to a spell to open the cover of this innocuous little diary.

"I could just ask it to open." I looked at Mrs. V for her reaction. She shrugged.

"I have tried to do that. You should do the same— perhaps only one person can ask it to reveal itself."

The box containing the fifteen talismans had only opened for me without a spell. It was possible this book was the same. After all, I'd been the one to find it.

"Please allow me to read the contents of this book. I am trying to protect the people of Henbane from someone who threatens our security."

Mrs. V took in a breath. I felt something wiggle under my hand. Like the book was alive—ugh.

"What?" I asked. "What did I do wrong this time?"

"Nothing. I'm just surprised at your wording," she said, her eyes focused on the book. "I did not think of invoking the protector angle."

I hadn't thought so much as just said the words that came to my mind.

"Try to read it," she said, nodding toward where my hand lay on the leather.

I lifted the diary and cupped it in my hand, spine down —just like Phillip showed me when handling delicate books. I opened my hand slightly, and the cover moved with me. The pages fanned open to reveal undecipherable scratchings on every sheet.

5

"Disappointing," Mrs. V said. "I suppose it was too much to hope that the first thing we read inside was 'the name of the killer is....'"

A joke? Another thing she'd never done. I was a bit off-kilter with this new version of my mentor, but I could get used to it.

"There's another spell," I said, still holding the book. "I can feel it. Should I order it to leave?"

"No. Let's try something else." She motioned for me to put the book on the table. "Perhaps you are feeling a preservation spell, and this is simply a code."

I didn't think so, but she knew more than I did about... everything. "If it's a code, D might have a program to try solving the key."

She walked toward her secret safe room. I stared at the pages while I waited for her to return. There were kind of patterns to the scratching, so maybe not magic to disguise the contents. Just because everything we'd touched so far was under layers of esoteric magical protections didn't mean this was.

Mrs. V returned with the bag of talismans. She'd taken them into her protection until I created my own safe room.

"Text Didier to come with his program," she said. "Meanwhile, we will work with these again."

I did as ordered and then put my phone on the counter, safely out of reach of any magical disaster.

"I thought we planned to wait until the festival was over," I said. "In case something goes wrong."

She tipped out the contents of the bag. Fifteen small objects, all with a symbol painted on the face. At least it looked like painting to me, but we really had no idea what they looked like. We'd only recently removed the first layer of spell—one that made the object look completely different to every person who looked at them.

"We aren't going to try to reveal all their secrets," she said. "Just one layer. I have a feeling that we can't wait too long. There are fifteen of these and we only have eight potential identities."

Her feeling was the same as mine, although I'd label my reaction as more like terror than feeling. We had seven more potential victims of this person behind the scenes.

"Is there any hint about how many layers are on them?" It would be nice to keep a tally, like we'd be more successful seeing our progress laid out.

"No." She was moving the talismans into a circle with a wooden stick.

My phone pinged. I walked over to the counter to see who was texting me. "D is on his way. Ten minutes."

"Then we have time to talk about our approach." She moved the book to the counter. "Didier can work here."

"Approach?" Up to now, we'd mostly just worked on a basis of Mrs. V telling me what to do and me following instructions until I got it right.

She sat down, the talismans now in a neat ring with none touching another. "Sit. I told you we were going to enter a new phase of your training. This will require patience and focus. I think you are ready to apply those even with a distraction in the room."

She let me digest that. I was going to do some pretty complex and dangerous spell with D working close by—in harms way. "I'll do my best."

"Yes." She told me to put my spell journal on the table outside the ring of talismans. D arrived as I followed the order. "We will get Didier set up, then proceed. While I talk to him, you will center your thoughts. This is something you need to practice. You will not always have time to meditate before casting."

Mrs. V took over instructing D while I listened and calmed my thoughts.

"I've found a suite of decoding programs," D said. "Let's see what we can get."

He took photos of a few pages of the journal and then got to work.

"Now your turn," Mrs. V said to me as we both sat at the table. "When spells are placed in layers, it is usually over time. I think with these talismans, the witch did it in one session. We haven't revealed enough to know for sure. If I am right, each layer removed will weaken the one below."

"So like doing it the normal way lets the individual layers cure? Like painting a wall?"

"An apt analogy," she said. The suppression spell was wearing thin enough that I saw the flash of pride in my progress. "We will also learn more about the reason to protect in this manner as the magic dissolves."

"Where do we start?" I wanted to finish working my spell before D could update us on his progress. Not because I was competitive—okay, not just because of that—I worried that I wouldn't be able to focus if D found something.

"It seems you are the only witch who can act on these items. Perhaps not just these, but that is for later. Your magic is maturing faster than I expected. Is your mind ready?"

Destroyer interrupted my pleasure at the compliment by saying, "Don't get ahead of yourself. You aren't a crow."

I refused to answer. I nodded and waited for her next instruction.

"Let's try a very simple approach first. Hold your hands over the circle and then put your power into the word revelare as you did before."

I swallowed and looked down at my hands. I spread my fingers to encompass the entire circle. I didn't reach for my magic, because I had no idea what that meant. I thought about what I wanted to happen, which was to remove the top layer of concealment, and said the magic word.

The symbols on each talisman squirmed and then straightened out.

"Well done." Again, she was radiating pride.

What had been thin and unrecognizable scratches thickened—not into symbols I could recognize as belonging to a particular witch, but into images we could research. I was proud of myself.

"Found something," D announced.

6

———

"Well, don't make us wait," Mrs. V snapped at D while she used the stick to push the talismans into the bag.

"It's not a lot, so don't be disappointed," he said. "There's definitely a confuse spell on the pages. Old and really well absorbed."

"We will attempt to clear it when we can focus," Mrs. V said.

I was a bit groggy from casting the spell, but I could feel they both generated waves of hope. We were making progress, and when I had a chance to restore my strength, I'd make more steps. Magic had never made me feel weak before, but maybe it was because of the muffling spell. Like the power had to force its way through to the world. Or... Mrs. V said my powers were maturing fast. Did that translate to burning out? Was I going to lose my magic? I couldn't ask the question because I couldn't face one more look of pity or frustration at my lack of knowledge.

"If it's under a spell, what kind of progress have you made?" Talking about this development might keep me from falling asleep at the table. Maybe I should ask about the effect?

"It's how the programs work," he said, pointing to his screen. "They're not magical. It doesn't mean the spell stops working—that would be a major disaster—but it sees the patterns. So I have a list of answers that might fit, is the best way to explain."

"Cossi, what is wrong?" Mrs. V asked. I guess she'd turned to look when I asked a question. A thread of worry curled around her head.

"I'm super tired," I said, keeping the fear that something was really wrong out of my voice—I hoped. I couldn't deal with another life-changing surprise. If I was losing my magic, then I'd have to go back to... well, nothing, because I hadn't started building a life after school. Of course, that thought brought me to tears. D and Mrs. V hurried over.

"Your skin is almost transparent," Mrs. V said, putting her arm around me and passing me a tissue. "You don't have that much color normally, but this is wrong. Do you feel any outside magic?"

Her touch helped. I hadn't noticed how cold I felt until she warmed me a bit.

"What is happening?" Destroyer screamed in my mind. "I will be there in moments."

I didn't have the energy to answer him.

"What were you doing before I came?" D asked. "Did she look okay before?"

Destroyer tapped at the patio door. D let him in, and my crow landed on my lap, his body nestled against mine. "I will make this better."

The warmth and presence of my familiar gave me enough strength to pass on what he said and answer their questions. "I was fine until you said you found something. I started to feel tired, but it got worse rapidly. Is it my magic?"

"Let me see," Mrs. V said. "Didier, make some restore tea. Crow, do not get in my way—perhaps you can watch over Tulip. I feel her getting agitated."

Destroyer mumbled, "I am not a babysitter," then he hopped off my lap and over to Tulip's basket.

"Pull the throw off my settee," Mrs. V ordered D. "It will do her no good to lie on the cold floor."

When I was flat on my back with her knitted throw between me and the stone floor, Mrs. V knelt beside me with a cushion to save her knees. "Phillip was ill. Have you caught his flu?"

I didn't feel like throwing up or sneezing or coughing. "I don't think so. I just got super tired."

The kettle boiled, and I watched D out of the corner of my eye as he poured water into the teapot he'd prepared.

"You should not react this way to casting a spell," she said, more to herself than to me. "Unless... well, a hex would do more damage. No. It is something much different."

She rubbed her hands together to warm them but didn't touch me as she ran her hands along my entire body. When she was done, D helped her stand. "She needs to drink the tea," D said. "And I've called Doc Rene."

"Can you get into the chair?" Mrs. V asked.

I nodded because I did feel a tiny bit better, and if the tea was going to help, I wanted it right away. I didn't even care what it tasted like.

"Drink," Mrs. V said, pointing to the cup D placed in front of me.

So I picked it up, pleased that my hand didn't shake, and threw it back like a shot of tequila. A light gingery, rasp-berry-flavored tequila.

"Well?" Mrs. V and D both stared at me like I was about to transform into some monster.

The tea suffused me with comfort. I was still tired, but I'd be able to make it home to bed. After that, we'd see.

"Better," I said. "What did your scan find?"

She sat and took my hand. Oh, this was going to be bad news.

"Your magic is fine," she said.

So why all the drama? Was it something more mundane? Was I dying?

"You are not allowed to die," Destroyer said.

"You are exhausted, but not under a hex. There is something changing in your powers, but I wasn't able to determine what. Tomorrow you must not ignore your need for rest."

"Where's the patient?" Doc Rene called as she rushed into the kitchen.

She checked me over and pronounced me healthy but tired. "A good night's sleep will restore you, Cossi. Tomorrow you must close your booth for fifteen minutes every two hours. Eat something, make sure you drink plenty of liquids—and that they're not all beer. I've been treating these symptoms all day."

She handed me an envelope containing a powder I should take with water to help me sleep. Then she swept out to her next dire emergency.

"See? I told you," Destroyer said. "I will sleep in the Protector's garden tonight."

I felt almost normal by the time D was packed up and ready to walk me home. "What did your program find?"

"Nothing but patterns, like I said. I've scanned every page and will keep going. But Phillip's name came up in several of the proposed decodings."

7

While we walked, D tried to explain the decryption process. It wasn't like I'd thought —that the program would read the screen and translate the information, kind of like from French to English.

"The book is a new language. Your power might not grasp it because only Martin knew it, and you need more context," he said. "If we're very lucky, we'll get to the translate step in time to solve the puzzle. It's more like AI. I have to teach it through feedback. So I'll look at what's been proposed and ask it to follow some of the clues."

"Like you tell it to put the mentions of Phillip in context?" I'd asked. I hadn't worked with any AI, as far as I knew, but I'd thought of it as a fast researcher that needed to be closely checked. That, in the absence of data, an AI would make something up.

"That's kind of right," he'd said. "I have to be careful not to bias it. So I can't say that where Phillip's name comes up, it had decoded it correctly, because I don't know if that's true."

Interesting. So more like an eager-to-please kid than a database. "Can you ask why it picked Phillip? Then use the logic to give feedback?"

"That's exactly the right approach," D said, beaming at me. "I'll ask why it came up with Phillip. Then ask what else the characters could mean, if there's context, that kind of thing. It'll take a long time to get there, but when we hit the right definition, the whole message will take seconds to decode."

After that, he'd gone home to engage in a conversation with an AI, and I'd come to the apartment to work on my magical knowledge. If someone could feed all the knowledge of magic at my fingertips into an AI, would it be easier to learn—or harder to be objective? Or would it simply reveal all of our world to another AI, one that plain humans used? I trusted that D had the right protections in place to keep the content safe from non-magical eyes.

I felt tired, but not so bad that I'd fall asleep right away. I needed to figure out a schedule for my booth tomorrow. Closing it every couple of hours seemed wrong, but passing out would be worse. Who would want to stay at a retreat run by a witch who couldn't take care of herself?

Phillip left me a note on the kitchen table that he'd retired early, so I was alone, and it was nice to have more space than just my bedroom—and to have a table and chair to use for study and planning instead of using my bed and falling asleep before I made headway.

I picked carefully through the tins of tea blends, making sure the one I chose had no trace of licorice—whatever Phillip used to suppress my power was heavily dosed with the tarry flavor of the root.

I settled on a nice raspberry and lemon blend. No caffeine, but also nothing to lull me to dreams too soon. I spread out the latest spell books I was supposed to be studying and placed a single plain sheet of paper right in front of me. I liked a list, I have to admit.

If I needed to make room in my day tomorrow to just rest, I needed a to-do of all the prep and scheduling. Ticking off an item always made me feel like I'd accomplished a huge feat.

To minimize the risk of forgetting to drink water, I'd take a large jug of it with me. I kept up the brainstorming until I had ten items on the list that would allow me to take five- or ten-minute breaks.

Tomorrow I would have all the energy I needed to cast spells.

When I underlined the list, I still had half the sheet to fill. I glanced at the books, dreading the boredom of theory. I was too tired and too distracted to study. Mrs. V might not agree, but I needed a night off.

My phone pinged with a text as I was shoving the books into my backpack for tomorrow. I could study in the booth.

The text was from Mark. *Too late to call?*

Instead of texting back, I hit his number in my contacts.

"Hi," he answered. I could feel his exhaustion through the air. Or maybe I heard it in his voice. It wasn't exactly subtle.

"Long day?" I settled back in my seat. If Mark needed to talk, I'd stay up. It was far less effort to listen to him than to read dry spell research.

"We're going to have a few more long days until we're back to normal," he said. "I'm calling to ask you if you want to explore tomorrow before the festival opens. See the farms, and the part of the island you haven't been to."

I didn't have to think too hard. A little recreation before I hit the booth would make the day seem shorter—even if it was actually extending it. Doing something just for me, with a man I enjoyed being with, would boost my energy, not drain it.

"How early? And should I make breakfast sandwiches?"

He responded with a warm chuckle that took the sting out of his next words. "I think we both know Jan would be a better provider."

I mean, I know I can't cook, so he didn't hurt my feelings. "Good. I don't know what I would have done if you said yes."

"Meet me outside Jan's at six a.m. We'll eat, then get to the farms."

He hung up before I could ask exactly where these farms were hidden. I knew they existed because D's family owned one. I'd been around the island a lot, and there was nothing pointing to their existence.

8

W e picked up coffees and breakfast sandwiches before we left for our ride. Beulah and I followed Mark on the path in the usual direction toward The Inner Spell. I didn't ask any questions because I was looking forward to the surprise.

"We'll stop to eat in a few minutes," Mark called back to me. "The farms are about twenty minutes from the turnoff, but there's a nice clearing just as we head west."

I tried to picture the path I'd ridden so many times since my first day. As far as I knew, there were no side tracks to the west.

A few minutes later, Mark stopped and waited until I was beside him. He pointed to a bank of bushes—salal, by the look of them—the kind of leaves florists used in arrangements.

"Normally you wouldn't notice the turnoff because of the angle, but it's a wide path because the farmers use carts to bring their produce in."

"Why would the farmers put a spell on the entrance?" I

asked, because I could feel the whisper of magic. Those shrubs were an illusion.

"Only for the festival," he said. "Visitors tend to disturb the animals. The residents know better than to do more than visit a friend or buy a few eggs or whatever. Don't point it out to anyone, okay?"

I agreed and took another look around. Sure, when I was going to The Inner Spell or the Earth Witch village, the hairpin turn would hide the entrance, but coming back? I really needed to be more aware of my surroundings.

"I'm getting hungry," Mark said. "Let's go."

The clearing was right beside the path. More a pullout for passing vehicles than anything. The path itself was wide enough for a horse- or bicycle-drawn wagon, but not two. "When do they make deliveries?" I asked as Mark spread a blanket on the grass. When he stepped away, he held out his hand for the food. "I've never seen or heard anything."

"In the early hours. Unless you're walking around at night, you wouldn't know. Spells make it silent. Sit."

I lowered myself, expecting a bit of a lumpy seat, but the blanket was thick enough to soften the ground. I took my coffee and breakfast sandwich, then waited for Mark to join me. Now I knew where the path was, my desire for a surprise was satisfied.

He spread out the wrapping on his sandwich as a napkin, checked his phone, and then took a sip of his coffee. "So far, no serious incidents," he said. "Just a few people feeling the heat, and a few who enjoyed too many beers or ciders. No fights, nothing broken. Successful festival."

"Do people fight?" If you put aside the murders—okay, they were bad—the island was peaceful.

"Not like a fist fight," Mark said after swallowing his first bite. "Arguments that get out of hand. I usually have to separate a few passionate researchers who stand on opposite sides of a theory."

Good, at least I wasn't wrong about the island. When we dug out whoever was behind the murders, the violence would be gone.

"I need to tell you something," Mark said as he finished his meal. He gathered the wrappings and wadded them into a ball to put in the bag. "I haven't had one call from that person. It's like I'm free to do my job."

"I was a little worried they'd find a way to trap you again," I said.

I hadn't taken my suppression tea this morning because I wanted to talk to horses, cows, sheep—any kind of animal the farms had. It meant I could see his emotions and catch the scent. He was happy, I guess, is the right word. His emotions were peach-colored and tingled in the air. Great. A new facet of the power.

"I guess that's what's worrying me. I can't believe it's over. I keep double-checking my actions to see if they are really mine. I don't know how to stop that."

It sounded a lot like having your whole identity flipped on its head. I had a hint of what that felt like. "You'll get past it. You were doing a great job before, right?"

"How can I be sure?" he asked. "We don't know how long the controls were in place. What if it was from the beginning and just escalated when the murders started?"

I was wrong. My experience didn't even come close to his. "I think you have time to be confident again. I mean, there's been no murder. And we'll catch this person. Maybe when you know who it is, you'll believe in yourself again?"

He looked at me, and the doubt just floated around him like fog.

"There's nothing we can do about it," he said. "And it's only been a few days."

I didn't know what else to say. Reading what people are feeling doesn't give me any insight on how to heal damage.

"I'll be patient." The doubt fog thinned a little, so I held onto hope he believed we'd be successful. "I know you and Mrs. V are digging into the diary—and the talismans," he added as he folded the blanket. "What about that pendant? The one we found with Martin Light?"

I wasn't sure how he would feel about what we'd done so far. D was involved, but would Mark think he had a role to play? And was it too soon to trust him? I would ask Mrs. V if she wanted him to join us, but a little information should be okay. I mean, if the witch controlling him found a way to do it again, I didn't want Phillip's or anyone's name to be made public.

I used the packing and getting back on the path as time to think it over, finally deciding on what I'd say. "We haven't done the pendant yet," I said as we headed out. "D's doing some work with the diary. And the talismans still seem determined to hold onto their secrets."

"Don't tell me anything more," he said over his shoulder. "If I know names, I'll have to investigate. It's taking a lot of effort for me to stay out of it. My power isn't just a skill to investigate when I think a crime has happened. It's a compulsion."

I agreed, and we rode in silence the rest of the way.

I guess we'd taken longer in the pullout than Mark expected, because we only had a half hour at the farms before we headed back. I didn't mind. I got to talk to a horse who only wanted to discuss good places to find grass, a sheep whose mind was too flighty to carry on more than a few sentences on any topic, and one goat who stared at me from the middle of a yard and told me to stop bothering everyone.

Destroyer laughed at my disappointment. "Not all animals are as smart as a squirrel or mouse."

I didn't care. Now I knew where I could find them, I'd be back at the farms again. When the festival was over. Everything was on hold for these few days.

9

The morning trip refreshed me more than sleeping in could have done. The fresh air and new voices were like a magic of their own—one that even plain humans could feel. I'd parked Beulah and run quickly up to the kitchen to brew my muffling tea so all the emotions wouldn't batter me throughout the day. Now I stood in my booth, jug of water under the counter and bowl of peanuts ready to fortify me.

The crowds were a little thinner because a lot of workshops were going on around me. A few of the spell writing ones interested me, but I had a booth to manage. Next year I was definitely finding someone to switch out with me. I should enjoy the festival too, right?

I chatted with a few people interested in checking out The Inner Spell for experiments—what I'd intended the business to be when I started—and setting up a time to look through the chalets before they were ferried back to the mainland and their cars, and normal lives.

I'd need to arrange with the current occupants for a

viewing, but I didn't think that would be a problem. The morning of departure would give me a couple of hours to show off the experiment spaces and book people in.

Then it was back to my normal life too. Hanging with my friends and learning skills, not solving murders or conspiracies. If my third power could grant wishes, there would be no more big crimes.

I got a text from Lilibeth: *Four more familiar and witch pairings. I didn't think having a handful of new people would make so much difference. Looking forward to a celebratory dinner Tuesday night when we're back to just the residents.*

I sent back a happy face emoji and then placed my phone beside the jug and bowl. Too tempting to scroll for information on codes and layered spells if I left it out during the quiet times.

The sounds of fun around me changed to hushed whispers. Something was happening. I stepped through the side curtain and out to the pathway. A small crowd of people were standing to the side, watching Mrs. V walk along with Tulip held close to her body. The audience was rapt, like Mrs. V was the Pope and they didn't want to offend her by being loud.

I was most surprised to see a few residents in the mix—three of the farmer families with children in tow. I guess I'd gotten used to knowing Mrs. V was a celebrity for the off-islanders, but everyone I knew here just treated her like a witch who'd been around forever—respect, but not awe.

She reached me and came to a stop. "Cossi, you are looking much better."

"I took everyone's advice," I said. "I won't get too hungry or thirsty, and I'll take a few short breaks throughout the day."

"Is one of those breaks coming up?" She looked at her entourage and then back at me. "I would like to talk, in private."

It's not like I could invite her into the booth for a cup of tea. I had nothing to sit on or make tea with, come to that.

"I can shut the booth," I said. "Did you have a place in mind?"

I could hear Tulip purring. The fact she did that had thrown me off at first. I thought it was only something house cats did. What I couldn't do was talk to her when she was so content. I hoped she never realized that and used it against me.

"There's a seat in the food stall," she said. "Jan has it set up more like a beer garden, so we can sit and relax."

Who stole my grumpy mentor and replaced her with this... kind? No. More like less grumpy witch.

I pulled the cord that kept the front curtain pulled back. "What about your posse?" I wasn't trying to annoy her completely, but a little teasing wouldn't get me in trouble, right?

She turned to them, and I saw a smile lift her face. "I have Protector business to do. Perhaps I will see you later today," she said to them.

The small crowd drifted away.

"I suppose I need to set up a short session," she said as she led me toward Jan's food stall. "I hope you aren't attracting people who want to waste my time, like I'm some kind of guru."

And there she was, my mentor.

I ordered tea, because I wasn't going to stand in my booth with a buzz, and Mrs. V didn't drink alcohol often, as far as I knew. When I rejoined her at a café table toward the back, she placed a feather on the surface between us.

"That will keep people from hearing us," she said. "I want to give you an update on the committee. I didn't ask for it, but Jeffery insists on telling me how they are proceeding."

The committee was meeting to address a very specific problem. With all the plain human activity of selfies and entitled poking around, the risk that a paranormal human would be uncovered was growing. My very first guest, Zinnia Flor, had replaced Martin Light as the off-island specialist when he was murdered.

"Okay, do you want me to talk to the committee? Since I lived as a plain human for twenty years?"

She pursed her lips and gave me the narrow eyes. "For less than that," she said, when she deemed I was sufficiently cowed. "You were born here, don't forget that. And you have enough on your plate already. When the festival is over, we will be returning to your lessons and expanding our search for the clues hidden in the objects we've amassed."

The talismans, the diary, and the pendant—that sounded like a Narnia novel in my head.

"So how are they doing?" I asked, knowing it was useless to argue.

"I despair of them starting to find a solution anytime soon. Jeffery tells me they are still getting to know each other. They haven't even started listing the specific problems, let alone a solution."

If she didn't want me to help them, what could I say? That I agreed to some extent with both sides of that argument? I changed the subject. "How is Tulip coming along? I remember taking a while to mesh with Destroyer, and he is fully grown. A kitten—even a lynx one—must be a challenge."

"We are not meshed," Destroyer announced in my head.

The tea had no effect on the familiar-to-witch communication.

Mrs. V smiled down at Tulip, who was lapping tea from her saucer. "We are both learning. I must say, your language power is nothing to be envied. Tulip has no sense of when to be quiet. Perhaps Destroyer can help her to learn?"

I promised to ask when we were back to normal.

10

The day passed in another whirl of meeting people and talking up my business and others. Phillip had dropped off a list of books people could buy at the bookstore. I thought it would be more successful if he let me sell the books themselves, but he hadn't agreed, so I let it go.

I dutifully closed for ten minutes every couple of hours. I enjoyed the opportunity to look at more of the booths than just those around mine. The Earth witches had a whole nursery set up to sell cuttings and growing manuals. I waved to Valerie as I strolled by, but I didn't stop. My history with plants always ended in death. I overwatered dry-soil-loving ones and underwatered those that needed a lot of hydration. And I planted shade flowers in full sun, or full sun in the shade. Believe me, I wasn't doing it on purpose, but I felt the flora would appreciate me staying away.

By the time I cast the closing spell on my booth, I was tired—normal tired, not feeling used up and wrung out. The breaks worked, as did the water and peanuts. I was ready to face my lessons.

Jan called me over and handed me a paper sack full of food. "Mrs. V called in an order," he said. "I just made it."

I thanked him and headed back to her cottage. I could smell the warm saltiness of french fries and bacon. We were in for a big session if Mrs. V ordered carb-heavy food. She usually fed me a cheese sandwich and a cup of tea.

My power bloomed as the morning tea faded. A couple of witches were talking in a guttural language as I approached, and then it melted into English—or I started to understand them. I slowed my pace to hear more.

"I don't know why people continue to ignore the signs," the woman said. "It's hot, drink water. You're tired, sit down."

"That poor doctor is going to need a vacation when we're all gone," the man said with a sigh of frustration. "Well, we're fine. Do you want to go back to that shifter bar? I think the beer is best from there."

They turned toward the bike park, and I kept going toward my mentor. I thought it was odd too. I mean, witches aren't all 'my body is a temple,' but they generally seemed to take care of themselves. Or was that a Henbane thing? I mean, life in a city is hectic and lots of people are too busy to keep track of their bodies—maybe it was the same for paranormals.

When I arrived at Mrs. V's cottage, I went straight into the kitchen. She was setting the table, and when I appeared, she said, "set up here. We'll eat before we start. I will be back."

Tulip wound between my ankles as I unpacked dinner. I'd guessed right—BLTs and fries. The kitten was bigger, and I had to focus to keep my feet. In a few months, she might be too big for the cottage.

"She is worried," the sweet voice said. "You make her worry."

"There are a lot of things—important things—for us to do," I said, trying to soothe Tulip and avoid a scratch. "Soon we will find answers, and then no one will worry."

"The crow said you would fix things." Tulip swiped at my exposed calf as a reminder she wasn't a house cat, but a wild predator. "Get on with it."

I used a paper towel to wipe the wound clean while I called out to Destroyer in my mind. "Can you tell her there's no need for violence?"

"It's just a scratch, and she has a point," he responded.

So much for sympathy. I told him to go back to whatever he was doing and let us concentrate.

Mrs. V reappeared at that moment, holding a velvet bag. She placed it on the counter and told me to sit so she could look at the wound. "What did you do to make Tulip scratch you?"

Why was it always my fault when something went wrong? I told her the kitten was trying to make her feel better. "She's still a baby," I said, excusing the behavior. "She knows you're worrying about the future."

Mrs. V turned to Tulip and smiled—again. Not a sight I got to enjoy much. "Can you hear us when we talk?" she asked.

"No. I can hear her talk to me, but that's all. Can you hear her in your mind? Or can you understand her when she mews?" I didn't know how the familiar-witch bond worked without my powers. I guess I'd assumed that Destroyer and I communicated so well because of my language power. He gave a sleepy caw of pleasure in my mind.

"Is she talking when she does that?" Mrs. V turned back to me and grabbed my leg, lifting it to see how deep the scratch went. She pulled a bandage and a small bottle of liquid from the cupboard over the sink.

"Right now, it's like baby talk, but yes, it's talking. Like when Roy barks—I can understand him if he isn't just making noise in frustration."

"This will hurt," my mentor said right before cleaning the scratch with a liquid-soaked cloth.

She had understated the pain by miles. I almost blacked out at the rush of burning agony in my leg. Then, as fast as it came, it was gone, leaving me gasping from the memory.

"Kitten scratches are more likely to get infected," she said, dabbing the wound dry before applying the bandage. "It's clean now. Stop being dramatic."

I didn't trust myself to respond with the respect a mentor and the Protector of all witch and shifter kind deserved. I made it to the table without much of a limp—some of it an unsuccessful bid for sympathy. We ate, the food settling my nerves and chasing away the trauma from Mrs. V's ministrations.

When we were done, I put all the dishes on the counter and wiped down the table with a sage-infused water. We were about to do spell work, and the sage cleaned all traces of contaminants.

"Sit and center," Mrs. V said as she poured the pendant and chain in front of me on the table. "Do not touch the pendant until I say it is safe."

Over the next ten minutes, she led me through four layers of protection spells—on me, my power, the other living creatures in the house. Not just a witch and a kitten—there were always mice or spiders or the like around.

When she was finally satisfied I'd done every spell right, she allowed me to reach for the pendant.

It felt oily against my fingers. Like some costume jewelry

that has a slippery texture. I let the chain drop through my fingers so that the pendant was the only part in my hand.

"First, we will try the simplest method. Try to open it." This is what happened with the box holding the talismans. It was locked for Elias, but opened for me.

The pendant did not cooperate.

"So not keyed to you," Mrs. V said quietly as she thought about the next step. "Does anything feel familiar? You may have encountered the locking spell before."

"It's just slippery. I keep checking to see if my fingers are covered in some kind of oil." I rubbed the tips of my fingers together as I spoke. Nothing but skin.

"Has it always felt like that?" Her question snapped out at me, like I'd been keeping some kind of secret.

"Yes, but it's getting worse every time I hold it." How was I supposed to guess that was important? "You don't feel that?"

"So simple," she said, avoiding my question. "Wait."

Where was I going to go? She looked at Tulip and must have told her to get out of danger, because the kitten sprang to her basket.

I was afraid to move in case I was supposed to stay exactly where I was. Mrs. V left to go to her secret room—or that's what I guessed, because it was in the direction she walked.

Within moments, she returned with a small tin—the kind used to hold balm or wax—and a pure white cloth.

"You will wipe the entire thing with this cleanser." She handed me the cloth and opened the tin. "I cannot believe we didn't try this earlier. Keep an image of an open pendant the entire time."

I did as I was ordered. A few weeks ago, I would have asked how to create the image and hold it and clean at the same time. Mrs. V's training had answered all those questions in our first few marathon training sessions.

When I wiped the last link in the chain, I moved on to the pendant. The cloth was thick with balm, so I opened it and wrapped the oval object, then rubbed. "I can feel the place where the lock is," I said. I tested the edges and then pressed on the release. I didn't expect it to open, but it did.

"Good work," Mrs. V said when I told her the results of my efforts. "Place it on the table, then unwrap it. Time to see what someone wanted to hide."

The open pendant was typical of its kind, holding a tiny frame on each side. Two pictures. On the right was a young man, and on the left a young woman.

"That's Phillip," Mrs. V announced. "Who is the woman?"

11

"How would I know?" I knew she hadn't asked me; it was more a question for her own thoughts. "My question is, why is Phillip's picture in this locket? We've assumed it belonged to Martin. What if it fell off the killer? I don't mean Tony Reed—I mean the witch we're searching for right now."

"It puts Phillip's recent illness in a new light. Perhaps he is on the list of victims." She told me to close the pendant and put it back in the velvet bag after taking a photo of the two portraits. "Too many new questions for every discovery. We need to think on this."

She took the bag and headed to the storeroom. I glanced at Tulip, who was staring at me like I imagined a lion looks at a sick eland. "I'm not doing anything. It's just happening."

"You are here," Tulip snarled at me. She kept eye contact as she spread her claws and started grooming between the little barbed weapons.

Mrs. V returned with the bag full of talismans, turning to Tulip as she entered. "You are a brave familiar, but this is not our enemy."

"What did she say?" I asked. "Should I make tea?" I needed something mundane to do with this itchy energy.

"Nothing I don't already know about you," Mrs. V said. "Brew the cleansing mix. No sugar or milk. We have a long night ahead."

What happened to waiting until the festival finished? It didn't open until the afternoon tomorrow so people would be rested for the big party that night. If we stayed up studying mysterious objects for clues, I'd probably miss all the fun. But there were plenty of festivals in my future. Stopping this maniac was too important.

While I brewed the tea—a mix of herbs and Ceylon that filled the kitchen with a brisk energy—Mrs. V started setting up for our next go-around. The talisman bag went in the center of the table, very precisely placed with the opening down and the ties ready to be released.

"We'll drink in the kitchen," Mrs. V said. "I want to keep the protections strong, so no unnecessary items near the table."

I poured the tea into two mugs and waited. I knew this kind of ritual required specific pacing. If I started early, the whole thing would fall apart. And it would be my fault. I hated to think what Tulip would do to me if she felt she had real cause.

An inch inside the edge of the table, Mrs. V laid out a ring of pebbles, all shades of brown with white streaks. An inch inside that, a ring of sand, then a smaller ring of tiny beads, then a final ring of white feathers touching tip to end of shaft.

"Protections," she said. "To save you the effort of casting your own. I want you at full power when you try to lift whatever is still protecting the contents of the bag."

Tulip clawed her way up Mrs. V's long skirt and sat on

her lap. She glared at me and licked her lips. *Way to keep the vibe safe.*

Her eyes narrowed at my thoughts. I guess I didn't need to say her name for her to know I was talking directly to her. She turned back to the table and sneezed. The force of it made a dent in the circles all the way to the bag.

"She did that on purpose," I said, sure the looks had been a challenge.

"If she sensed something wrong, she was protecting us," Mrs. V answered, cuddling Tulip to her chest.

"Destroyer?" I thought to my own familiar.

"What?"

"Come and take charge of Tulip." I wasn't going to risk the spell failing because of her. Mrs. V seemed incapable of teaching the kitten any manners and always took her side.

"I am not a babysitter," he said. But then I heard a tap on the patio window.

"You stayed here all this time?" I asked. I'd been speaking my half of the conversation aloud so Mrs. V—and Tulip—knew what I was asking.

I slid the door open for him to walk in. "Take her to the yard and make sure she's safe."

Mrs. V chuckled at my attempt to be the boss with my crow. "I see I'm not the only one who is unable to convince an animal to be something she's not."

Tulip jumped off her lap and followed Destroyer outside. I hoped the tiny lynx didn't try to capture any local prey.

"She will be safe. Do not take too long. I have important business." Destroyer waddled outside and flew up to supervise from a branch.

12

"Do you have any advice on training her?" Mrs. V asked. "You have had your familiar for more than a month, and he is not marauding."

"If only," I said with a sigh of regret. "You know he's decided to take on the role of crow emperor of the universe, right?"

She grunted a laugh as she reset the rings of protection. "There must be a way to form a working relationship. If I can't tame her a little, I will need to move to the solitary villages for everyone's safety."

We both sat again. I wasn't yet ready to try something as risky as we'd planned with the talismans. A conversation about familiar management was just the thing to clear my mind.

"She's a kitten," I said. "That means something. Her mother sent her to you very young, so patience might be good. How much do you talk to her?"

Mrs. V looked up from her preparations. "It depends what you mean by talking. I tell her how pretty she is and cuddle her, like a kitten."

The world tilted as I took that in. Mrs. V—the grouchiest woman I'd ever met, the Protector of the paranormal world —cooing over a tiny predator. I clasped my hands in my lap to avoid holding onto the table for stability. Then I heard a chuckle from Destroyer that reminded me I chatted with a crow all day.

"You need to teach her the rules," I said. "Talk to her like a companion, maybe? She's not a cute, cuddly domestic cat. She's a wild creature with all the instincts to protect her pack and fight for survival. Maybe taming her isn't the right goal."

I held my breath waiting for the reprimand. It was the first time I'd said anything like that to her.

"Worth considering. Perhaps I should be working toward an understanding of how to live within a community." She made the final adjustment and then told me to clear my mind.

It wasn't easy the second time. I took three deep breaths, but my day still buzzed in the back of my mind. I could also feel the talismans, like a greasy smoke invading my thoughts.

I didn't want this power. Understanding all languages was great. Reading emotions from people—and a few animals—was a mixed blessing as it moved through my senses from knowing to seeing to tasting and then smelling. The taste of sorry was so bitter I needed honey to clear it out. Now I could see spells too. What would a bad spell smell like? I could hope that burning tires was the worst of it.

I knew I should tell Mrs. V. Maybe it wasn't just me. Maybe some spells exuded a threat. I assumed it was a threat—happiness and delight wouldn't manifest as greasy smoke crawling toward the feathers. The smoke didn't quite touch the first protection ring, so it was working.

I told her, because I couldn't do this without help.

"That's not normal." She peered at the bag as if she could see the effect if she only looked hard enough. "We need to get on with this. The rings won't last forever."

That thought joined the buzz of worry in the back of my mind. "This is going to take a minute," I told my mentor. "Is there something I can do to chase the last tinges of worry?"

She looked at me, and I prepared myself for a lecture—but it didn't come.

"Is the teapot empty?"

I'd made the big pot, so the answer was no.

"It's not going to taste as pleasant, but it will help." She filled my cup with the new, over-brewed and cold liquid.

I could smell the bitterness and a little rot. She handed me the cup and told me to ignore the smell.

I blew out the air in my lungs and tossed back the entire mug like it was a dose of medicine. I felt my brain swirl—not like I was dizzy, but like it was being flushed. Then a moment later, my thoughts were clear, and I was ready.

The smoke pulsed at the line of feathers, but nothing new happened except I didn't feel dirty. Some part of my mind was barring the spell from entering.

"What's the approach?" I asked, because I wanted this done in one go.

"The same as before. I want you to use that persuasion power to clear the last layer. Not a nice request. An order. If it works, we will have made a step forward in our investigation and gained some knowledge of the extent of your magic."

Easy for her to say. She wasn't the one using forbidden powers.

I reached and loosened the ties on the bag and lifted it so the objects fell in a small pile. The smoke flowed back and spread through the pile like some kind of mold. I told the smoke to leave. It curled tighter to the stones, becoming part of them. That wasn't what I wanted.

"The spells that cover these objects are not wanted. I command every concealing magic layer to disperse and reveal the true talismans." I thought the intention at the pile. Nothing happened.

I thought my words were strong enough. In fact, I found them weirdly supervillain in tone—who was I to command anything? As I started to come up with another way to demand I get my way, the smoke rose in a whirl, lifting the talismans enough to click them against each other. Then the stones fell back on the table in a pile, and the smoke was sucked out like we had an industrial extraction fan running.

13

Mrs. V took in a sharp breath. "This is not good."
She didn't have to tell me that. I could feel the wrongness emanating from each of the stones. Now that we'd cleared all the layers, we had fifteen ovals of deep black stone. Onyx? Basalt? Something I'd never heard of? They shone like a glow stick lived inside them. Each had a clear symbol carved into the face—Valerie's turtle, clear as day. D's dad's albatross. We'd be able to identify the owners of every one of them. I reached out to touch one, hoping to learn more by feeling it.

Mrs. V slapped my hand back. "No. We need gloves. These are hexes."

Every organ in my body dropped. The one thing I'd thought was a constant had just been ripped away. Magic was only cast for good—using it to hurt anyone was dangerous for the witch who did it. A wave of anxiety rolled through me. Every time I thought I was clearing space in my mind to go forward, something dragged me back under a pile of complications.

"We should destroy them," I said, in a much squeakier voice than normal. Fear did that to everyone, right?

The patio door rattled, both familiars fighting to get inside. Mrs. V let them into the kitchen.

"Do not put yourself in danger," Destroyer cawed at me as he flew up to land on my shoulder.

I heard Mrs. V tell Tulip not to worry.

"Why shouldn't we worry?" I asked. The squeak was gone, but the fear stayed. "What can these do? How do we dispose of the hexes? Isn't it illegal?"

She looked at me, and I saw the annoyance rise from her body—at me, at the situation, at having to deal with two animals. Then it faded into something more like acceptance. If that was even an emotion.

"We will pick the hexes up when I bring the protective gloves. They will likely only affect the intended victims anyway, but we are going to be extremely cautious."

"If these are the real objects, then how do we get rid of the magic?" I couldn't pull my mind back from the idea that we had some kind of bomb in front of us. The only way forward was to defuse it. And the timer was approaching zero.

"That we will do when we know more," she said. "Try to calm yourself, Cossi. This is not the end of the world. Hexes have been cast before, and the world still exists."

She picked up Tulip and took her along as she headed for the secret magic storage room. Not so secret to me, because I had the key to unlock it—but to everyone else. It was where she kept evidence from cases Mark solved, because she is the island's crime lab. Where she kept secrets related to being the Protector. And dangerous magic.

"The Protector is right," Destroyer said in my mind,

much calmer now that he knew I wasn't going to grab a handful of bad magic.

"This could be the last piece of information we need to catch the person behind every murder," I said aloud, because I needed the comfort of the idea. That this was almost over. One more step and I'd be back to what I'd come to believe was normal. Running my business, hanging out with friends, exploring Henbane, and learning. No more deaths. No more investigations.

"Yes, it could well be," Mrs. V said as she came back with two pairs of gloves. Not latex ones, but cotton, infused with protective magic. "You will examine each piece in turn. I will record the emblem, and where I can, the name of the witch."

"We know these two," I said, pointing to the turtle and the albatross. "When do we destroy or deactivate them?"

She placed Tulip on her cushion and told Destroyer to find a perch out of the way. Then, drawing a notebook and pen out of her pocket, she settled back. The table was still ringed in protection, and the stones remained in a pile.

"Deactivate first," she said. "Until we know the owners are safe, we cannot risk destruction."

I didn't think these belonged to the witches identified by the carvings. They were the victims.

Mrs. V wrote the two symbols we knew on a blank page —one column for the symbol, one for the name. "Pick up Valerie's and tell me what you can learn."

That started the process of reading each hex. It didn't take long, but by the end I was sick enough to need a remedy. Something about residual magic.

On her orders, I arranged the fifteen hexes in a circle close to the feathers. "Can we remove all the hexes in one go?" If we had to do it one at a time, I wasn't sure I had the energy—but I'd gladly burn myself out to free the victims.

"No. We don't know what will happen," she said. "We need to do it one at a time."

The recent murder victims all had hexes, as did the killers—well, Carly's, the shifter who died after committing murder, was linked to her mother and inherited by her.

"One of the murdered witches? Or one of the prisoners?" I yawned after asking and patted my cheeks in an attempt to extend my alert time.

Mrs. V didn't answer. She looked at me, then at Tulip.

"The Protector wants me to tell her if you are too tired to continue," Destroyer said. "I am not a go-between."

That was a bit of a surprise—not that Destroyer was too important to stoop to messenger, but that Mrs. V had realized the familiars could be used to circumvent any attempt at lying.

"Tomorrow," she said. "Early. I do not wish this to fail because you are not willing to manage your energy."

My phone buzzed, cutting off my retort. I retrieved it from the counter. "Mark. He wants me to call him."

14

I considered putting the call on speaker, but maybe Mark was reaching out for a social thing, and I wasn't ready for Mrs. V to comment on my dating life.

"Cossi," he said when he answered. "Where are you?"

There was an urgency in his voice that told me this wasn't a dinner invitation. "At Mrs. V's. Working magic stuff." Until we had results beyond exposing fifteen dangerous objects to the world, I'd keep our work under wraps.

"Good, you're safe there. Those talisman blanks," he said, with a little hesitancy. "Do you have any left?"

He wasn't asking because he wanted one. Something was wrong, and I knew it had to do with the people who got sick. I should never have believed it was just a lack of self-care. Even if Doc Rene assured me it was. My heart started racing again. "There are a few left in the bowl," I said. "In the booth. Why?"

"I need one to test," he said. "There's a problem."

"Go ahead and get one." He could enter anywhere as the cop—my booth would be fine. The closing spell would reactivate after he left, so I didn't have to be there. "Am I making people sick?"

Mrs. V looked up from her notebook, but I was too focused on the call to wonder what she was about to say.

"Did anyone mess with the talismans?" he asked, in that infuriating cop way of ignoring my question.

"Phillip checked the ones I had left—no magic on them. And I didn't put any on there. I just cut and sanded them before drilling a hole for a chain or something. What happened?"

His voice changed, and I realized he was inside my booth. "We found one with a weak spell on it. To make the holder forget to take care of themselves. Like someone was trying to sabotage the festival. Where's the bowl?"

There was no magic on the blanks. I repeated that to myself as I pictured closing out the booth. "Under the shelf, maybe. I might've put my scarf over it."

"Got it. Give me a second." He must have put the phone down because his voice faded. I heard him say a few words —a spell to check for evil? "It's clear. Someone added the magic after you gave the blank out."

"It wasn't me." I heard the defensiveness in my voice. I didn't care. If people thought I had something to do with all this illness, I didn't know how I'd face the community again.

"I know," Mark said. "I have the altered one, and now I'll check deeper. It doesn't feel like your magic. It doesn't feel like anyone's magic."

"Should I recall them?" Tears were starting to fill my eyes. Why would anyone do that to me? Just when I was feeling like I belonged, some witch snatched it away.

"No. Between Doc Rene and me, we can neutralize them without causing a panic. No one is going to blame you."

"Who would do this?" I asked. "I mean, everyone loves the festival. Is it because I brought new people here?"

"Stop looking for ways that you are to blame for things you haven't done," Mrs. V snapped at me. "Tell Mark to bring me the altered piece when he has a moment. I may be able to track the witch who cast the spell."

I did as ordered and ended the call. Destroyer told me to stop being an idiot and get on with my real work.

"It's too much of a coincidence," I said to Mrs. V. "How many people would cast a hex? Even a mild one?"

"That is the right question. You are too tired to continue. Place those things in the bag. I expect you back at first light."

"Why not keep going?" I wouldn't be able to sleep with all this running through my mind.

"Exhaustion equals mistakes," she said. "I will make you a tea to take with you. Go to your room as soon as you arrive, drink the tea when you are in bed. Sleep."

I just obeyed. Not even a mental argument. Sleep was the best way to recharge, and without the tea, I'd be fretting over every unanswered question. Tomorrow, we had the whole morning to work with the hexes before the festival opened.

15

I woke up to the sound of birds. The dawn chorus was usually a little muted, but today it sounded like every single songbird was outside my window. I was fresh, rested, and ready to save the world—thanks to the tea. I guess saving the world was more about figuring out who on Henbane was casting hexes.

Despite the internal worry that I'd made some kind of horrible mistake, I knew my blanks were safe when I handed them out. Mark would find out who tainted them, and we'd deal with it as soon as we had some proof.

I'd be back with my friends by the end of day tomorrow. I'd missed them—Lance was with the pack, under Dolph's orders to make their part of the event successful. Lilibeth was working long hours at her pet store, boarding pets and matching familiars with witches and helping Doc Rene, and D barely had time to join me for a quick coffee—or beer—between managing the various technological disasters and decoding Martin's book.

I know in the rational part of my mind that I wasn't alone. The thing is, my rational mind had no sway over my emotional one. In my heart, I felt like I'd been abandoned, with all the problems on the island weighing down my body.

I did my morning routine, which included filling my backpack with everything I'd need until tomorrow—snacks and a full water bottle for the booth, my spell journal, my latest reading (we probably wouldn't get to studying, but I didn't want to get caught without homework), and a bag of the tea to muffle my powers.

Phillip didn't come out of his room while I bustled around. He needed rest if he was going to get better, so I left him to it.

When I got outside, my stomach rumbled. I hoped Mrs. V had bread for toast—then I caught the scent of rosemary roasted potatoes and bacon. Jan was open for the early morning trade. I popped in and ordered two breakfast buns and a coffee traveler.

"Long day," he said as I waited. "You should be resting or you won't enjoy the party."

"Mrs. V doesn't take a day off," I said with a laugh. "And why are you open so early?"

He called an order into the kitchen and rang up a bill. "The people setting up for today and tonight need sustenance," he said when he was done. "How could I sleep when people need food and drink?"

Our magic powers made us do things. Not bad things— that was the human in us. Jan's power as a kitchen witch would make him feed people in need. I wasn't sure what his other powers covered, but I'd bet it had something to do with harmony, from the way he always found a way to balance my fears with hope.

"I heard another witch got sick," I said, hoping he'd be able to fill in some details—although another part of me didn't want the link between my swag and illness to be general knowledge.

"Yeah. Mark found a hex on the wooden charm holders you were handing out." He picked up the order from the kitchen and delivered it to a table of solitaries in the corner. When he came back, he leaned on the counter and looked into my eyes. "You are not responsible for what happens after you hand over a piece of wood."

Maybe not in other people's judgment—but in mine, yes. "How do you know I'm not the one who put it there?" I hoped really hard that he'd have a concrete answer. One that would lift this blanket of guilt.

"Mrs. V would know. She's your mentor, so she's aware of everything you cast," he said. "And you're not the hexing kind. That magic bounces back too easily."

Had I just wished him into saying that? My third power sometimes acted on my needs rather than on my orders. But he'd said Mrs. V would know. There was no way she'd keep something like that to herself.

"I didn't know my magic reported to my mentor," I said. "Now I'm rethinking every spell I've cast."

"And feeling guilty over the ones you didn't really need to?" He grinned at me in solidarity. His rueful emotion came through in a lilac haze. "We've all been there. I know it's hard to do, Cossi, but let Mark figure out who's behind the hex. I mean, it could be a kid, right? Testing out a little prank. I promise no one thinks it's you."

My order came up, and Jan put it in a bag steeped in a keep-warm spell. The traveler of coffee came with cups and stir sticks. Like everything on Henbane, they were compostable, but I declined.

"Mrs. V insists on real mugs and plates. Thanks for the boost. I'll try to stop feeling responsible for everything."

Something told me I'd never be able to drop any of it. I'd spend my life picking up more and more burdens along the way.

He waved me off and turned to the next customer. I walked to Mrs. V's cottage, trying to convince myself to believe him.

16

Destroyer was in the backyard with Tulip when I arrived. He was on a branch watching her, and she was curled up in a sunbeam, sleeping in that way babies, puppies, and kittens do—all loose and relaxed beyond reason.

"What happens when the festival is over?" I asked Mrs. V as we enjoyed breakfast. "I mean with the residents. Do we all sleep for a couple of days?"

She poured honey into her coffee and stirred it with a collectible teaspoon—this one had a castle at the top of the handle. It looked top-heavy and clumsy.

"No. Life returns to normal. Nightlife dies down for a few days, I suppose, for us to recharge. What do you really want to talk about?"

I don't know why I tried to ease into anything. I asked her about the monitoring of my magic. Still a bit of a delaying tactic, but I needed the answer.

"Are you afraid of me finding something out? Are you casting spells I need to stop?" She took a big bite of her sandwich, so I had to answer—because she couldn't speak.

That was a bit of a cheat. I wanted answers, not interrogations. "Fine. No, as far as I know, I'm not casting spells that will harm anyone. I don't know if my power to convince people to do what I want is acting without my knowledge—like before we knew what it was. All those times when I got what I wanted and figured it was luck. That was my power, right?"

She put the sandwich down, and I got a pale yellow wash of sympathy—definitely not what I expected.

"Your power has been muffled during the day," she said quietly. "Have you wished I would do something in the times we've been together?" A smile grew on her face like she already knew I had.

"Sure, but it never worked." The light started to dawn on me. "So I can wish for something without worrying I'm coercing someone?"

"I cannot be sure, because we don't make a habit of suppressing powers without the approval of the witch involved. I think before we knew about it, your power was trying to break through Phillip's spell. Now that it is free, you must specifically apply it. Does that align with your experience?"

I'd missed the fact that my power was dulled. I mean, I knew the language and emotion ones were because I missed them. But I guess I was so used to not using the third one, I didn't notice. "Now you put it that way, yes."

"Good. Then we should start our work today." She finished her sandwich and moved the plate and coffee mug to the counter, giving me a look that said, are you going to waste more of my time?

The answer was yes—but calling it wasting time was a bit harsh. "One more question," I said, moving my plate and mug to the safe zone. "People trust me, but they don't know about my third power. Isn't that going to smack me in the butt when they find out?"

Of all my powers, the third worried me most. The language power seemed stable, the emotions kept changing like they were evolving to my needs, but the third one? I still had no idea if it was working when I didn't want it to. I agreed with the rules on this one. What kind of witch would I turn out to be if I could get my way without any effort?

She took the bags of protection circle ingredients from a drawer. "Not if I have made the decision to allow you to keep it. The Protector makes the rules, Cossi. I took an oath to protect our world—it's too important to just leave it to chance that a Protector wouldn't turn evil without a binding. I have enough wiggle room to allow you to keep using your power, but that is probably the extent of my discretion."

There was more, but I could tell from the midnight blue suffusing her emotions that the discussion was over. Whatever secret she kept would come out when she was ready—or never.

I washed my hands and waited until the pebbles, sand, beads, and feathers were back in place. Time to do the hard work of identifying both the witches or shifters who were hexed—and the witch who cast it.

17

"We will work on one hex at a time," Mrs. V said. "Do you have a preference?"

What would I base my choice on? We knew a few of the names. Would it be better to experiment on one from a murder victim—limiting the harm it could do, but also limiting how much we could learn? Or try to identify a whole new witch? I asked Mrs. V what she thought.

"What will we learn from a dead witch's hex?" she asked in her teacher voice. Not reprimanding me for sloppy thinking, but pushing me a little further down the path.

"Who cast it?" That really was all we could hope for. "What happens when we identify the person who cast the hex? Can they remove them?"

"I would not trust such a witch to do so," Mrs. V said. "Now, what can we learn from identifying a live victim? And what are the risks?"

I thought it through. If we identified a new victim, we could talk to them and then remove the hex and see the results. Then we might be able to ask them who cast it—

without killing them. When I had it sorted out in my head, I told Mrs. V my conclusion.

"If that person is on Henbane now, that would be a good approach. What would we find if we chose one from a murderer?"

It wasn't like we'd identified every owner, so this could all be just a thought experiment. "We might be able to identify the purpose of the hex, and the witch who cast it."

"Is that helpful?" she asked, as though there was a real answer.

"To some extent," I said, this time doing the thinking aloud. "If we know what the hex is, we'll know if removing it will cause more harm. Is that possible?"

"Everything is possible. What other way might we find the author of the hex?"

"It bounces back," I said. "Someone will feel the results of us removing it? Wait—could it be several hexes?"

"I only feel one spell over the objects," she said. "I leave it to you, the decision. Choose someone deliberately, which means we first identify the remaining victims—or leave it to chance. I'm not sure we want to risk Valerie's life, or Didier's father. Rothtect is not on Henbane yet. Using his symbol means we will not see the results."

Picking someone did feel a little like I was deciding who to jeopardize, but leaving it to fate was still a decision. If the outcome was bad, I would still feel responsible. The only aspect I could control was time.

"Chance," I said. "I don't want to wait until we've found all the owners. Every second that passes while we try to identify witches is time for the person who cast this to harm someone."

She smiled like I'd done something right. All I'd done was make one choice out of a list only consisting of bad ones. I wasn't used to her showing approval, so I didn't spoil the moment by asking questions.

"Reach into the bag without looking and pull out one talisman." She settled back with her notebook on her knee, ready to record whatever disaster happened.

I cleared my thoughts—okay, mostly doubts, which were the worst thing to take into magic casting. When I was ready, I opened the bag and slid my fingers inside. One oval seemed to jump into my grip, and before I could overthink it, I pulled my hand out.

The symbol was a cluster of berries. "Who is this?" I asked.

"I do not know all the symbols," Mrs. V said, with her usual snap of annoyance. "We will add that to your curriculum. Witches have many symbols, not just one."

"It kind of looks like currants," I said. Maybe if we knew exactly what plant it was, it would give us a clue.

"Or soapberry, or any number of other edible or poison plants," Mrs. V said, waving off my attempt to dig deeper. "What do you feel on the object?"

I knew better than to call it a hex before testing to see if more spells existed. When I revealed the hexes, we'd stopped. I'm not sure if it was shock or something diverting our attention, but I should have looked deeper right away to see if the hex was layered over an existing talisman.

The hex oozed on the oval like oily smoke. I opened my power just a crack to read any emotions. Yes, the rings of protective magic blocked the power from automatically reading the spells. I hate to think what I'd do if I were suddenly overwhelmed with evil pleasure. That's what I got from the hex. Whoever cast this hoped it would get triggered. This wasn't a precaution against being caught—it was a time bomb.

I gritted my teeth and forced my power below the murk. Hope.

"The talisman wasn't created for the hex," I said, with a sigh of relief that took some of my fears with it. "It was taken and polluted by another witch. I don't know whose it is, but we should be able to lift the hex. Perhaps then we'll know."

I placed the talisman in the center of the rings and slammed the door closed on my power.

Mrs. V was making notes in her book. Not on the table she'd created, but on a clean page. I couldn't read it all, but I saw my name. Recording my abilities?

She looked up and frowned at me like she was wondering how far we could push before we broke something.

"Tea," she said. "Thinking tea. Come to the kitchen."

I was glad of the break—and if there was tea to help me think, I wanted the recipe.

18

She opened three different tins—tea leaves, dried rhizomes of turmeric, and one of rumpled peppermint leaves that immediately lifted my spirits with the sharp scent.

When the tea was ready, she poured us a mug each. We hadn't talked the entire time. I didn't know what was going through her head, but mine was creating ever more dire consequences of lifting the hexes.

"Think about what you felt and saw with that hex," she said when both mugs were empty. "Was this image of the berries under, over, or part of the hex?"

Apparently, the magic in the tea worked fast. My mind zeroed in on the memory. I hadn't consciously noted the details, but they were there.

"Over," I said, eyes closed to keep my thoughts from scattering. "I can't tell if it's similar to the original or even if there is a symbol under it. I thought we'd taken all the layers off." I opened my eyes, hoping to see that rare smile again. My mind was still filled with vague and dire scenarios.

Mrs. V was making yet another note. I didn't keep such

detailed records. Was I supposed to? Was this something she'd be annoyed about when we were finished with this current crisis?

"This is a very skilled witch," she said, without looking at me. "Someone is hiding their abilities, because I should know if a witch capable of this is living here."

Ugh. Another complication. "What should we do next?"

She glanced at the table, then back at me. "It would be safer to stop."

What the heck? "And leave this witch to kill again? To keep the rest of the people in their control—to suffer?"

She smiled at me again, like I'd passed some kind of test only she knew about. "Ask your familiar. If we go further, it will endanger you—and because of your link, him."

I didn't need to ask. He was already talking in my mind. "If someone is threatening my realm, they must be stopped. I prefer you do it without dying, but an emperor protects his subjects."

I passed on his comment.

"Then we continue?" she asked.

I nodded, because I couldn't quite get the words out. It was kind of scary that she was letting me make such important decisions. More than letting—she was pushing me to do it. Was this a secret test? To see how long it would be before I made the wrong choice?

We sat in our places at the table. "So how do I remove the hex?" There must be a way for any witch to do it with a spell. Maybe it wasn't all up to me.

"You will remove one of the protective spell objects. There are three extra pebbles and a cluster of the beads. Do not create a gap. When you have them all in hand, place the pebble on top of the hex, the beads in a circle around it, the sand must be covering all of the components. I will give you the words to use when that is done. Then use the feather and the words to clear away the magic."

Not too complicated, and with all the instructions, I knew how much to take from each ring. One pebble, enough beads to create a circle, enough sand to cover them. I carefully collected my ingredients, leaving a scarily thin line of sand behind, and followed the instructions.

"Use the power of persuasion to enhance the spell. We have too many to clear for you to use only the innate power of a witch. The words are: 'I command the evil to return to the caster of this spell'. Don't waste time with your usual worrying."

It seemed a bit vague, but without names, there was nothing we could do. I did as I was told, adding a little force to the words.

The air filled with the acid reek of burning tires. I stifled the cough, afraid it would break the spell. When the hex dissolved, we were left with a clean oval of jet black with a tea leaf in the center.

"Leanne Macy," Mrs. V breathed the name.

The amulet melted into a pool of ink, then dried on the table.

"Put everything away," Mrs. V whispered. "Leave the remains of Leanne's hex. We will purify whatever we clear when it is done."

A shivery blue emanated from her. Not exactly fear, but maybe she was trying to hold that back. I didn't ask any questions, keeping all my focus on safely tying the pouch and clearing the four protections. The sooty remains held no hex, but magic always left something behind.

When we were done, Mrs. V poured rubbing alcohol over the top of the table and set it on fire. Before I could run for the extinguisher, she killed the flames with a muttered word. No evidence of any damage to the wood—but also none of the hex.

The questions I'd smothered came rushing back. "Will that happen with all of them? What if Mrs. Macy wasn't dead?"

Mrs. V gave me a stern look that broke the spiral of panic.

"Sorry," I said automatically.

"Never apologize for wanting to learn," she said, keeping

her eyes on the table. "My knowledge of this did not increase with the removal of the hex. I need to do much more research."

She took my gloves and the pouch to her safe room. I mean, that's what I thought of it as. Not to protect the occupant from intruders, but to protect the world from the contents.

While she was gone, Destroyer tapped on the patio door. "The kitten needs food," he said. "I cannot stop her from terrorizing my army. She is undermining my authority."

Trust him to brighten my day. I opened the door, and Tulip leapt over the threshold like it was an abyss—then lost her footing and slid onto her side. And like every other feline, she got to her feet, shook off the memory, and walked with dignity to her food and water bowls.

"I'll talk to Mrs. V." I hoped their connection could blunt the predator in her familiar. "I'm surprised you need help handling a kitten."

"Keep her fed, and she will only pretend to hunt," Destroyer said as he flew up to my shoulder. "You did a very good job in removing a little of the evil from the world. I am proud of you."

"Do you know anything about hexes?" I never knew where his knowledge ended and his disdain began, but it was worth a try.

"Only that they taint the world." He pecked at a curl and pulled it like a rein. "Go back to your festival. Let the Protector solve the problem."

I would love to do as he suggested, but I couldn't run away. "You should go back to your... what are you doing while the festival is on?"

"Training and resting. I will come if you need me." He

launched himself from my shoulder in a low swoop that took him through the patio door and out of my sight.

"It will take me time to find the right volumes," Mrs. V said as she returned with three heavy ledgers under her arm. "You may ask two questions before you leave me to it."

For her, that was generous. Until today, if she didn't want me around, she just ordered me to leave.

"What should I be looking for?" I figured the death of the hex should have some effect on the witch who cast it.

"There may be no repercussions. Leanne is not alive to feel the benefit. If someone is suddenly weak or ill, keep an eye on them. Perhaps have your crow tell Tulip, and she can pass on the information to me. Next question."

It was hard to choose one that didn't require her to research for an answer, but one thing was weighing on me. "Did saying her name make the hex dissolve?"

"No. It was coincidence. A lot of coincidence. You choosing a hex at random that belonged to a dead witch— and one that I knew the symbol used beneath the foul magic." She placed the books on the table and sat. "I will let you know when it's time to come back and finish the work."

I went to the booth and opened up. It was a little quieter today—I guess people were resting up for the party tonight. The feeling that I'd left something important undone sat in my stomach like a hot chili.

It was the hexes, and I knew we couldn't blindly go ahead and lift them all. There was always a risk of actually killing a witch every time one melted. It was different now that I knew those talismans were hexes. I felt the weight of responsibility to free people from their influence without doing more harm.

"You look like you're solving the world's problems," Ms. Flor said as she stepped up to my counter.

My first and favorite resident at The Inner Spell, she was working with the council to solve the problem that constant selfies and livestreaming posed. I guess that was an oversimplification, but the paranormal world got closer to exposure with every picture blurred by magic.

"Just the usual," I said. "How is the committee going?"

"Slowly, but that's to be expected. We spent a whole day getting to know each other. Today we're trying to pinpoint when the risk began to grow. I'm arguing that it started the day someone first posted a picture on Facebook—so about twenty years. Others think it began a few years earlier, but most of us agree the whole world changed when the internet was unleashed."

There was that timeline again. Something did happen that long ago—my mother made her mistake. Did it weaken the protections worldwide? Was Henbane, and other isolated communities, the only place where the shield recovered afterward? No paranormal would post a selfie of their meal, or a view, or whatever. But in the wider world, perhaps that second of revealing us was the first step in erosion. Or maybe it was all a coincidence, and the committee was right to blame the internet.

"Will knowing when it started help bring it to a stop?" I wouldn't work on the problem that way. I'd look at all the evidence of weakness and then solve the problem—but I wasn't part of the committee.

"Probably not, but we need to feel something solid in our work. It's very overwhelming for the Henbane witches. I'm beginning to wonder if one off-island representative is enough."

"Why don't you suggest someone to invite?" I asked. Living as a plain human for most of my life so far gave me a unique perspective. I sympathized with her. It was a huge load to carry.

She checked her phone for the time. "I have to go back. I promised to bring refreshments. Let's get together when everyone has gone back to their normal lives." She floated off, waving to a few people as she headed over to the food tents. Zoe was providing food today, with Jan and Sheena on the bar.

I saw Doc Rene in the distance headed toward the

medical tent. She was helping a witch as they went. It reminded me of the call from Mark. My bowl of blanks was now empty. I didn't have receipts, because there was nothing to sell this year. I had my memory, and I should be able to come up with a list of people who took one of my giveaways.

I mean, it had been three days—how bad could my memory be? I remembered a few people, but most of them were off-islanders. Buddleia Twotrees and Phillip were the only ones I could name. And I could see her over at the weaving workshop, looking healthy. Phillip was sick, but it started long before he touched one of my pieces.

I made a promise to myself to check on him today, just to make sure he was still getting better.

21

On my second break, I was so worked up about Phillip that I ran over to the bookstore to check on him. It bothered me that I seemed to be the only person worried that he wasn't getting healthier. Maybe it was a witch thing—that they didn't get sick often and didn't understand how quickly a cold could turn into something deadly. I was used to plain human diseases—the kind that killed old people. Phillip might not look it, but he was over a hundred years old. In my mind, that meant vulnerable.

The bookstore was closed, a sign on the door announcing evening hours. Okay, that made some sense. The festival probably disrupted the routine for everyone. I ran around the side of the building to the street door leading to the apartment upstairs.

He was in the kitchen, making tea—rose hips and mint. He looked dreadful. The bruise on his hand was fading to the yellow and purple of healing, but the flu was holding onto him like a leech, sapping his strength and turning him into the old man he really was.

"I thought you were getting better," I said as I stood in the doorway. I didn't want to catch whatever he had.

"I simply need rest," he said, his voice thin. He pulled his sleeves down to cover his hands, then adjusted the hood of his robe to cast a shadow over his face. "This illness is poorly timed. I am missing out on the festival, and yet I'm not able to sleep. The bookstore needs to be open."

Being the only person to run a business meant you had no one to take over when you needed to be elsewhere—like in bed recuperating. But Phillip wasn't alone.

"I could run the store," I said.

I didn't want to, but the booth had served its purpose, and I'd only had one person drop by for directions in the last two hours. Phillip had done a great job teaching me his business, even if he'd been a terrible mentor for my magic.

"It's only another two days," he said as he wafted the steam from the tea toward his face and made his way to a chair. "Not even that, to be more precise. I will close the store the moment the last boat ferries visitors to the mainland. I will sleep for however long it takes. I am only glad that I have not infected anyone else."

I recognized that stubborn feeling of independence from my own history. I hated when people fussed over me when I was sick. I told him to sit at the table while I went through the cupboards. We were low on comfort items.

I made a quick trip to The Basics—Effie's grocery store —for lemons, honey, and a balm the clerk recommended.

"I'll check on you tonight," I said once I'd put away the supplies.

"No, enjoy the party," he said, drawing his cloak closer. "I will close the store early and go to bed. You can't miss your first festival party. Especially this one—the end of summer is the most fun, and who knows what next year will bring?"

He wouldn't let me argue, threatening to place a lock spell on the doors to keep me out. He tried to laugh as he said it, but it ended quickly in a wheeze.

"I'm telling Doc Rene," I said. "If I come by and the store is open too late, I'll call her to come cure you with some awful-tasting concoction." He'd been grouchy for days, but he was sick. I didn't have an excuse to be anything other than cheerful.

22

B y the time I got back to the booth, the crowds were already drifting toward the center. A bonfire was stacked and ready to light later, and people were taking their afternoon snacks with them to stake out a good spot for the show.

My neighbors were starting to shut down, and I checked to see if anyone was still heading our way. Nope. I could spend the next hour standing alone—or I could close up too. Not to head to the party, but to return to Mrs. V and continue our work.

My phone buzzed as I tidied the pamphlets on my counter into a pile. Zinnia Flor.

She didn't wait for me to say hello. "Cossi, thank goodness you answered."

"Is something wrong?" I pictured the entire committee succumbing to the taint on my handouts.

"No. Yes, but not wrong wrong. Can you come and talk to the committee? We're having some challenges communicating."

"You mean, they can't grasp the problem?" I asked with a

laugh. With only Zinnia's voice as the sole off-island witch, I could imagine the disbelief she faced. Plain humans were complicated—and at the same time, pretty simple. And they had no idea what was hidden from them as they made their way through life.

"Exactly," she said. "Can you come?"

I had to give it a try. As diverse as the plain humans are, their response to learning a whole magical world existed wasn't hard to imagine. And it wasn't all smiles and open arms.

"I'll be there in ten minutes," I said. "I need to close the booth."

She thanked me and ended the call.

I'd go to Mrs. V after the meeting—and after I ran by the bookstore to make sure Phillip closed up and rested. Why did every action I needed to take come with so many before-I-dids?

The group was still in the business center. I tapped on the door and waited to be let in. I knew everyone around the table except Sexton Bold—a shifter who had only returned to the island a few days ago.

As I scanned the group, I realized D's dad, Batiste Roth-tect, was still missing. I'd forgotten that he was still recovering from food poisoning and had kind of expected to bump into him somewhere. He'd spent a lot of time in the world beyond Henbane, so he'd be able to add his experiences—and Sexton should know what Ms. Flor was saying was real. He'd been off-island for some time too. Was something else going on? Like a touch of magic keeping the committee stuck in the early phase?

"Cossi, please tell us about your experiences in the plain world," Effie said.

"It might help if you tell me what you're having difficulty

with," I replied. "Maybe I can clarify what Zinnia has already told you. I'm sure you don't want a recounting of my whole life until a month ago."

"She tells us that plain humans have lost the little respect they had for privacy," Valerie said. "That they think nothing of asking people to stop what they're doing in order to take a video that they will publish on TikTok."

I looked at Sexton, trying to understand why he couldn't explain it.

"I did not interact with the general populace," he said, as though I'd spoken aloud. "Had I known we would be in this situation, I would have made more of an effort."

I guess I understood. He was focused on what he wanted —not on an exploratory mission into the effect of social media on human societal norms.

I thought carefully as I answered. "It's not a lack of respect," I said. "It's not all humans, but the ones who try to make their lives into a... commodity are unaware of boundaries."

"Really?" Effie said. "Come on, Cossi, you aren't going to be reported for frankness."

I guess it was an old habit—not giving offense, often to people who didn't think twice about offending everyone within sight.

"They don't understand that other people are living their own lives. They act as though the world—no, the universe— is there for them to use. It's not that they want to be disrespectful, they just are. And remember, they don't know we exist. This is our problem, because we can't let them find out. The behavior of a few people is simply an annoyance to most humans."

The six sets of eyes stared at me—even Zinnia, who lived among plain humans.

"No wonder we are unable to grasp the problem," Sexton said. "You have given us a lot to think about. Thank you."

"Perhaps we need Cossi to join us after all," Valerie said. "But we must wait until Batiste joins us before we propose changes."

"And Patience will need to approve it," Effie added. "She is, after all, the girl's mentor."

Mrs. V has a first name?

23

I didn't mind missing the party—well, not much. Our work with the hexes was vital, and if we were successful in releasing the victims, I'd have the rest of my life to party. Okay, I guess either way I'd do that, but cleaning the taint of evil magic off these witches would let me do it without a skim of guilt. These hexes were definitely not my fault. Leaving them active would be—and as long as these existed, witches were in danger.

D joined us with his laptop and printouts of the images he'd taken from Martin Light's book. I guess we had two tasks tonight.

"Put the journal aside for now," Mrs. V told him. "We start with the hexes."

She placed the bag in the center of the table, the drawstring pulled open and facing down. For protection this time, a multicolored braid circled the table—leather strips dyed green, yellow, and lilac. I could feel the power emanating from them, even through the effect of the tea that muffled my powers.

"You are safe," Destroyer called out in my mind. "The Protector built a strong barrier."

I thanked him without asking what he meant. *No distractions.*

"The braid will enclose any reaction," she said. "Since you don't need to touch the objects, you will be safe if it's activated."

I had an image of my fingers being sliced by a whip of leather protections. I sat on my hands, until I had to act.

"I want Didier to see the symbols," Mrs. V said. "He may be able to use his computer to help us identify our witches. When we are ready, Cossi, you will shake them out."

"What if they all fall face down?" I wasn't ready to start flipping the ovals over, given the risk of finger shortening in the name of safety. Let alone the nauseating idea of actually touching a hex.

D shook his head. "Unlikely. The odds are that some will be face up. We can start with those. I'll need to see them to decide how to proceed."

"Do you have a list somewhere of witches and their various symbols?" Mrs. V asked, keeping her eye on the bag as if it were an unruly student in a classroom. "Or a way to compile such a thing?"

D pulled a fourth chair over to use as a desk. He opened his laptop, and I saw a screen full of icons. "No. I mean, I don't have such a database, but I'll be able to search for images. You might even recognize some, right?"

If she did, Mrs. V hadn't mentioned it last night. But maybe she was biding her time, gathering more information before revealing what she knew.

"Cossi, take the bag. Please make your mind clear first. I don't want you open to any contamination."

I was getting more efficient at getting my thoughts to unscatter—if that was even the word. I closed my eyes and waited until thoughts began to coalesce in the darkness. I thought at them to leave, and in moments, my mind was ready.

I pulled my hands free and snatched a corner of the bag, lifting and giving it a little shake to make the contents pour free.

D's prediction came true. Of the fourteen hexes, I counted ten face up. The symbols were clear. I put the bag on the counter and returned to my chair, sitting on my hands again.

"Do you have any thoughts?" D asked. "Where to start? Even what information we're trying to access?"

Mrs. V glared one more time at the hexes as if to scare them away, and then turned to face me and D.

"We have two people who have agreed to be test subjects. I contacted a guard at the prison last night on a... hunch." She said the word like it was a curse. "Both Tony Reed and Billy Fern. I thought I recognized the symbols from a long time ago. Tony is that cog, and I'd be surprised if there wasn't a star cluster on one of the face-down hexes."

The cog was in the center of the pile. I'd need to separate it from the pack to work on it. "Will the gloves still protect me?"

She passed me a pair, and I slid them onto my hands.

"Do not remove the object from the protections," she said. "And do not do anything until I say we can start."

I wasn't exactly burning to reach into the center of a pile of hexes—protection ring and gloves aside.

"Okay," D said, looking up from his laptop screen. "I've set up a database to fill. I've added the symbols we know— Leanne Macy, murdered, tea leaf. I think we know Dad's is an albatross from earlier. Valerie Nightshade, turtle, and now the two new ones. All this might help us find the remaining connections."

Mrs. V accepted the information without comment. "We will start with Tony. If we succeed in not killing him, you will need to turn all the hexes face up. We will move on to Billy if his is there, and then we will see."

I figured the other option—if we killed Tony—would mean we had to stop and regroup. AND DEAL WITH THE GUILT OF MURDERING HIM! Even if he'd agreed to be a test subject. I guessed the other possibility was that nothing would happen.

"If it's successful, why wouldn't we just keep going—at least with the ones we can match with a witch?" I really wanted this to be over.

"Because I need you at full power. I'm not saying we'll stop, but if you try this level of spell too many times, you may burn out. No one is helped by that." She turned to D. "Have you recorded all the symbols?"

"When the others are turned over, I'll add those. But having ten images will help me search for answers. It might be nothing, but of the ones we know, only Tony's is face up."

"It is not nothing," she said, without adding more. "Start your searching. We will work on our part."

I thought back to the way the hex had reacted last night. The effort it took to clear Leanne's hex wasn't much— mostly the gross smell of the burning power. "If it works the same, we'll need to clear the table after each hex we remove."

"Worry about the first part," she said. "No, not worry. That would affect the magic. Focus on Tony first. We will decide how to proceed when that is done."

I looked at the hex. It was the same oily-smoke-covered stone as the one before. Despite Mrs. V's order, I could try something different. If my power of persuasion was the key, surely I could order it not to dissolve. Taking out a deactivated hex rather than cleansing the table would be much faster. And having the stone might teach us something.

I couldn't risk the protections by removing all the other objects from the table, so I used Tony's name as a focus as I took all the steps to remove the hex—and keep it from dissolving.

The smell had us all coughing, but it worked. Tony's inactive stone sat where the hex had been. I reached in quickly and placed it on the bag, not in.

24

"Are you going to call the prison?" I asked. I mean, the whole reason to pick Tony's hex was to find out what happened. "Before we do anything else?"

She nodded slowly, like she was thinking deeply about the decision. "First, let's see who else might be under a spell. I am less concerned about Billy since he is safely under observation. I think it would be prudent to learn who on Henbane is at risk of becoming a murderer."

I hadn't even thought about that. I'm so stupid. Billy and Tony were both in prison for murder, and we think they might be the weapon rather than the actual killer. So one of the remaining hexes could be used to drive another witch to commit all kinds of crimes.

"I'm ready," D said. "Turn them all face up and I can do some quick research while you get ready."

Mrs. V looked at me like I was the one in charge. I was sure to get it wrong. After all, I'd only been a witch for about a month—yes, I'd always been one, but I didn't know, so it doesn't count.

"Let's be very careful. I don't need my power refreshed to turn the objects over, but these are hexes. Should we limit the number we take out? Like minimizing the potential damage?"

"Now that the layers are removed, I think that's a good step," Mrs. V said. "We may have been lucky before when we tossed them around like playthings. Three at a time. Leave the protections in place."

I could see the fear vibrating around us—not just from D or Mrs. V. I could see my own anxiety blending in. Another new thing. I'd never been able to see my emotions before. Along with all the worry was one sharp orange spike of anger. Coming from Tulip—I ignored her.

"Just the images." I didn't want to awaken any weird magic by keeping the hexes out of the bag while we identified the targets. Who knew if saying the name would trigger the spell?

We worked fast, and in ten minutes we had the list of images. Only fourteen, since we'd destroyed Leanne's. We already knew D's dad, Batiste, was the albatross. Valerie's was a turtle. Tony's was a cog. Now we needed to link the remaining eleven to names.

The hexes were all safely back in the bag, and D was typing away on his laptop, looking up meanings and whatever else he could find for clues to the identities.

I sat back and called out to Destroyer, "Does the all-powerful crow emperor have any insight?"

It was more to hear his grumpy voice than an expectation he'd give us answers. I missed his presence. I knew he'd be back in a day or two. The visitors would be gone, and the animals would get back to normal. But he was my familiar, and I was kind of jealous of Mrs. V and Tulip. They'd stuck together the whole time.

"We do not meddle in such things," he said, adding—just as I was about to bring up the shiny objects I kept finding on my windowsill, "not sparkly enough."

"Tea," Mrs. V said, pushing up from the table. "No food until we are finished with these beastly hexes. I don't want you vomiting on my floor."

Nice. I guess I didn't want to get sick either. So far with the two I'd deactivated, I hadn't felt anything, but two hexes with a gap between them was very different from thirteen all in one session. I figured once we started, we'd keep going until everyone was freed.

Mrs. V was texting someone when the kettle boiled. I took it off the burner and swished hot water around to warm the pot. She'd measured out the leaves, so I set it to steep. A warm honey and sharp lemon scent filled the kitchen. All three of us sighed like we'd dropped a heavy sack.

"Good, that worked," she said, putting her phone down. "Heaviness tends to build slowly and subtly. It's important to approach darkness with a light heart."

I was thinking it would be better to approach clearing hexes with speed and knowledge, but I was grateful for the lift in spirits.

"The guards inform me that Tony is alive and reports feeling like he's stepped from his foundry in full burn into a crisp spring morning. I think we are safe to remove the hexes without informing anyone they were under one."

"I have some names," D said. "Not all of them, but most."

"We will start with Billy Fern," Mrs. V said. "If we are right that he was under a compulsion, then it seems only fair that we release him from it now."

"And from prison?" I asked.

"He and Tony are safer there until we find who cast the hexes," Mrs. V said. "Who else is on your list?"

D turned the screen toward us. Jeffery Peak, Azalea Pink, Alder Bark. There were more, but I stopped reading. "Why them?"

Mrs. V sipped her tea and waited for D or me to work out the reason.

"They are influential," D finally said. "Important to the community, on the council. In fact, they may know more names. Should we ask?"

"Not yet," Mrs. V said. "Here is what I propose. We clear Billy. Then we invite Jeffery here. If his memory is affected by the hex, it would be useful to know."

"And if he suddenly remembers something, we could have our answer." I didn't know what to hope for—that Jeffery got his memory back and told us who cast the spell to break it, or told me why this was all my mother's fault. Or that his issues had nothing to do with the hex.

It didn't matter in the long run. We were going to lift these hexes as soon as we knew who the symbols belonged to.

"Get Jeffery to come," I said. "We can deal with Billy's, then move on."

25

I t was getting later in the morning, but I still had a few hours before I needed to open the booth—if I was even going to bother.

Jeffery agreed to join us as soon as he could get away. Apparently, the committee was in the middle of a brainstorming session.

We couldn't ask Billy about the hex, in case he died trying to tell us—like the other two murderers. The guard did confirm his symbol: a star cluster. Billy had been drawing it since he arrived.

"That will speed things up," I said as I dug into the bag for the right hex. "Maybe as we free people, they can identify more."

I placed the hex in the center of the table and straightened the gloves.

"We will test the protections when you are done," Mrs. V said. "If we are successful, I do not want to pause to refresh them."

I agreed. The faster we got this done, the better. "Maybe do it after we've released Jeffery? And the other ones we know—Batiste and Valerie? Should we ask Doc Rene to be with her?"

"I'll let my mom know we're going to cast a spell," D said. "Not what it is—I like having a dad, and I prefer to keep him alive. He's still in the hospital, getting better, but the doctor isn't ready to release him yet."

"You think it's the hex?" I thought it unlikely. Unless Batiste was the one who cast them in the first place. No—why would he have one if he made them?

"I don't know." D wrinkled his forehead in thought. "I guess if he has a miraculous recovery? Being under a hex could drain you. If you get sick, it's worse."

"Stop guessing and get this done," Mrs. V snapped.

Did one of these belong to her? No—she would have known her symbol, right?

"I've sent Doc Rene over to Valerie. No details. I just said it was Protector business." She nodded to me to continue what I was doing.

We were set. I cleared my mind—it was getting easier each time. I focused on the hex on the table, a star cluster scratched into the center. Billy Fern. He could go back to being that nice man I first met. He didn't deserve to be in prison because of a compulsion.

I reached for my third power—okay, it's more like just thinking about it, no mystical reaching out. The hex cleared in a puff of acrid smoke. The stone, now innocent, went with Tony's. I wasn't sure how we were going to dispose of them, but I doubted anyone would want to use them as talismans again.

Mrs. V's phone pinged with a text. "Billy is fine. Also says he feels like a load has been lifted. He doesn't know anything more than he did a moment ago."

D was still typing away, looking for symbols. He hadn't

heard from his mom, so I guessed we would wait on that. Still—two more hexes we could clear in the next few minutes. Leaving ten.

"What's the impact on the witch who cast these? As we remove them?" Everything I'd learned told me there would be one. A backlash—and for this kind of spell, it would be bad.

"I've never dealt with anything of this magnitude," Mrs. V said, checking her phone. "There will be something obvious. It may not happen until the last one is clear. Doc Rene is with Valerie."

Jeffery arrived as she finished. "Stay in the hall," Mrs. V ordered. "We cannot have you disturb the balance."

"Right. What do you need?"

She asked him if there was some image he used to identify himself. A bit vague, but good enough considering the risk of death.

"I used to have a magnifying glass. On my books. To make sure I could prove they were mine."

"That's all we need. Wait there." She raised her eyebrow at me—because I guess I didn't move to the bag fast enough.

"Should he sit?" I asked as I put the hex in place. "I don't relish trying to move him if something happens."

"Didier, go be with him. And Cossi has a point. Use the parlor." She waved her hand at me to get on with it.

I was getting faster at this with practice. In a moment, we were clearing away the burning-tire reek. This time my power felt different. Maybe just being able to use it consciously was strengthening and deepening my knowledge. When I didn't know I was using it, I felt nothing, obviously. At first, it was a thin wisp of heat. Now, when I used it, my body kind of warmed up all over.

D came back without being asked. "He's fine. Do you

want to talk to him? And Mom said she's with Dad, so go ahead and do what you want."

Mrs. V looked at me. Was she letting me decide?

"We only know two symbols." I tried to get her to say something, but she wasn't in the mood to help. "Batiste is in the hospital, so there's help if he reacts differently. I mean, he's sick, so maybe it will make it worse—or better? Valerie is the same, but she's so much older. Although she's on the island."

"Are you asking?" she snapped at me. I guess she was expecting more, but I didn't have a single real fact to work with. She frowned, then waved like she was chasing away a gnat. "Trying to find the right answer is a waste of effort. Go into your heart. Look for the answer there."

My decision was going to be based on a guess—I didn't hold out much hope for my heart. I asked Destroyer, but he had no advice. I looked at D—it was his dad, after all.

"We've done three, and it's been fine," he said. "Dad is strong."

I closed my eyes and let my mind clear. When it was done, I had two names—no surprise.

"I think we start with Valerie. Doc Rene can tell us right away if something is wrong. Then we do Batiste. He might not feel the effects right away." *How was I so sure about that?*

"Didier, tell your mother to be ready. I have alerted Doc Rene." Mrs. V nodded toward the hex bag.

I pulled out the turtle stone and placed it on the table. Then I went through the process, remembering to hold my breath this time when the hex burned off. As soon as it was done, I pulled out the albatross stone and repeated the spell. Now we'd freed every witch we could identify. A sense of satisfaction filled me. We'd cleared a third of the hexes.

"Valerie had a bit of a dizzy spell, but now is telling Doc Rene she feels ten years younger."

"Mom says Dad's fever is going down." D looked at me, the relief painted across his face and emotions both. "I didn't want anyone to know, but I was really worried."

"Jeffery, come in," Mrs. V called. "Don't let Tulip out."

26

W hen we explained what we were doing, Jeffery sat with a plop. "How many more witches are under this spell?"

"We still have nine symbols to identify," I said. "It's proving harder than I hoped."

"Let me see." He leaned forward and stared at me like I was his savior.

"Did anything change when we first lifted the hex?" I asked, hoping he'd say that his memory was whole and he knew everything that happened—and who kidnapped him.

"The darkness is less apparent," he said. "Not gone, but not so much in contrast. I have not been struck with all the memories—yet. I hold out hope. A feeling I didn't realize was missing until you freed me."

Well, I guess we can't expect everything to improve. I mean, the witch behind it is still out there. I poured the remaining hexes out and turned them face up. It was much less intimidating to see so few left.

Jeffery leaned even further in and squinted at each one in turn.

"Alder and Violet Bark," he said, pointing to the lavender sprig and the twig. "The book must be Lawson Quisk, and I think we all know a witch who loves a cocktail."

Azalea Pink. The hex could explain her constant tipsiness. Day drinking would explain it too, but people also drank to get rid of feelings—for a little while.

"One at a time? Or should I try all at once?" I was asking Mrs. V, but I'd be happy to take anyone's answer.

"How are you feeling?" Mrs. V asked. "You need to be strong either way. And it will take me a moment to reinforce the protections."

"I can help with that," Jeffery said. "Or I can make a restorative tea."

"I'll keep looking for names," D said. "From the parlor. This room is getting a bit crowded. And I'm not sure I can stand another lungful of burned hex." He gathered up his laptop and headed out.

And no one had taken the decision. Rats!

"Destroyer," I said aloud so it wouldn't look like I was ignoring everyone.

"What?"

Grump. "Am I affected by removing the spells?"

"Why are you asking me? You should be able to tell how strong you are."

"I feel like I can do all of them at once, but I wondered if the hexes might be making me overestimate my ability. Like a trick to make me screw up."

"Smart. Yes, you can. Do it all or only the named witches."

I thanked him and passed it on to Mrs. V and Jeffery.

"I am reluctant to release unknown witches," Mrs. V said. "I've sent a text to Mark to bring everyone we've identified to Doc Rene. They're all at the festival, and he will notify us when they are ready."

"It is also good to manage the process on the hexer," Jeffery added. "I want to speak to him or her. If we suddenly release the entire batch, we may never get that chance. But this discussion is better held over tea and a few cookies to celebrate when the deed is done."

Good. I decided to do one removal spell. One more eye-burning reek and four witches freed.

"Now that we know more names, is there a connection between the people we know?" I'd spent a lot of time trying to find a link that would give us an underlying motive.

"Over tea and cookies," Jeffery repeated. "I am anxious to see how this works."

While Mrs. V and Jeffery worked on the pebbles, beads, feathers, and sand, I sorted the hexes. The ones we'd cleared, I put in the pottery bowl. The unidentified ones I left in the sack. When I was done, I pulled the ties and double-knotted them, as if that would stop any bad reactions.

Mrs. V's phone pinged. We were ready for me to do the biggest neutralization yet.

I pushed aside the worry about having an audience in Jeffery, the fear I'd hurt one or more of the witches—and the dread of what might happen to the hexer with the release of four at once.

My body filled with reassurance and warm power as I thought the order to dissolve.

In seconds, we were choking on the fumes. Jeffery dispersed the smoke and then opened the patio door to bring in some fresh air.

"Mark says the witches are fine," Mrs. V said. "I'll make the tea. Cossi, you clean the mess."

27

A fter tea and a short rest, we were no further ahead. Jeffery couldn't remember anything new, and he said the symbols felt like he should know the people attached to them, but he couldn't connect the memories.

It was going to take time. We couldn't go out asking people at random if they recognized symbols. One of the remaining hexes could be a decoy to alert the person who cast the entire set.

Jeffery nodded toward the sack. "My instinct is these witches are all influential—and that's why they are the victims. Someone wants their power. Perhaps they haven't used that power, but just having the potential is worrying. It's a good way to force witches to do little things against their will. Small things often build into larger ones over time."

"Maybe the murders are just a coincidence?" I asked. "My instinct is it's all part of the same thing. But I could be wrong." I didn't think I was. Not because my gut was infallible, but because there was heat in my entire body when I second-guessed myself. Like my magic was trying to burn the doubts clean.

"Too many unanswerable questions," Mrs. V said. "Everything points to more research."

Another delay.

"I should go open the booth," I said. "Let me know if you think of anything."

"Be alert," Mrs. V said. "For anyone suddenly ill or showing signs of weakness. Perhaps we will get some good luck. I'm not sure how long we can spend time looking for a villain. They must know by now that we have released so many of the hexes."

"Are we in danger?" I asked. I couldn't leave if either of them required protection.

"I think it will take time for the witch to find us," Jeffery said. "When they do, we will be at risk—but they will be weakened."

It wasn't exactly a 'don't worry about it', but I knew pressing the point would have no effect. My mentor and Jeffery were both better at using their power than I was. And both of them were radiating a steady green determination.

I HEADED TOWARD THE FESTIVAL, trying not to stare at everyone on my way for signs of a hex bounce-back. All the witches I passed looked tired but excited for the upcoming party.

"Cossi!" I heard my name and turned to see Lawson Quisk hurrying across the street. The committee was still meeting in the business center, but I expected them to stop soon for the party. It was a pity they had missed so much of the festival.

"Taking a break?" I asked.

We stepped aside from the growing flow of witches into the festival grounds. It felt like every witch and shifter on the island had decided to have lunch at Jan's or Zoe's and were now looking for space to sit for the rest of the day and night.

"We are about to shut down until tomorrow," he said. "I had the oddest feeling a few minutes ago. Like someone had lifted a veil from my eyes. Not that I can grasp the reality that Zinnia continues to tell us is true. Perhaps it would be simpler to find islands for all the witches and shifters in the world."

I didn't mention the hexes—I didn't want to start a panic. But it was great to hear him say he felt suddenly clearer. And since he was in good health, I guessed he couldn't be the caster.

"I think it's probably too late for that," I said, hearing the regret in my voice—and weirdly feeling it in my bones. "Too much is mapped and constantly under satellite images to give hundreds of communities a chance to find havens like Henbane."

That made me wonder what satellites do see of Henbane. Maybe it's too small to notice, or somehow hidden? Or maybe something more? My brain started to melt trying to sort that out. A question for D—when we had nothing more urgent, like finding the witch who cast the hexes and figuring out what to do with them and the two witches currently in prison.

"We remain stuck trying to understand the problem," Lawson said. "It may be too late when we finally grasp the extent of the danger."

I'd been in group work like that at university. Someone —or more than one someone—always thought getting the fine details down first would help complete the project faster. Usually a few in the group, like me, would just get on with it while they split hairs.

"Would it be useful if I came in again and tried to help?" It was getting too late to open my booth anyway, and it would be easier to spot a sick witch at the party—or figure out who wasn't there if I wandered around.

"Yes, if you would be so kind. I think we should be talking to Patience about using your skills. Surely your mentorship has moved along enough for her to spare you?"

I followed him to the business center, trying not to giggle at the sound of Mrs. V's first name.

"Ah, Cossi," Zinnia called when I stepped through the door. She was tired, frustrated, and relieved. I hoped I could come up with something to deserve her faith in me.

Seeing her emotions so clearly reminded me that I hadn't refreshed my muffling tea. I guess not being surrounded by the sight of people's emotions had worn away some unconscious coping mechanism. As much as I wanted the peace, I'd have more luck finding the culprit with my powers operating.

"I've done some facilitating," I said. One of the courses at university was all about focus groups and meeting management. I had no idea it would come in handy in my new life. "Tell me where you are in the process and I'll try to help you move forward."

As I suspected, they'd spent the entire three days trying to understand the various ways plain humans intruded on paranormal life.

"We can't retreat like those of you here and on the other islands," Zinnia said. "We have lives. We've built communities. Uprooting might just expose us by our absence."

I listened for a few more minutes while the others tried to explain what they didn't understand.

"What if you just believed her?" I asked. The room filled with a pink aura of shock. "Not that you don't—I mean, instead of trying to understand. Take all her stories as facts. Try to remember the plain humans aren't trying to find the witches and shifters... yet. We have time."

Effie looked at me, her emotions mixed up but vibrant— much like everyone in the room. I was starting to get a headache from all the emotional reactions in a small space.

"So, as an example," she said. "This problem of plain humans taking photos of everything—and some artificial intelligence, whatever abomination that is—putting the blurring together is the problem. We need to find a way to, I don't know, vary the obscuring spell? That way it won't be able to find a pattern?"

Abomination was a bit strong.

"Yes! Exactly that. Like if the magic was set to provide an image—what the plain human sees would be best—then the AI wouldn't notice anything."

The group started talking among themselves. I smiled. They'd taken on a huge problem as far as I could see, but maybe the solution was a simple spell.

I slipped out and left them to the discussion.

28

I headed for my booth. The mass of witches and shifters was gathered at the center, waiting for the fun to start. I decided to clear the contents and take them to my room so that tomorrow I'd just have to take down the posts and roll up the fabric for storage. Although, I guessed there was probably a spell to do that for me.

My headache from the committee's emotions had eased a little, but with so many people around, it was hard to block out all traces. At least most of the crowd was excited—a few just trying to last long enough for the party—but not one negative emotion floated toward me.

"Coming to the festivities?" Mark asked, startling me back to reality. "The party gets going in a couple of hours."

I'd promised D I'd go with him, but that was before he started decoding the diary. I wasn't planning to stop figuring out the hexes for a party. I was pretty sure D wouldn't take a break either.

"We've made some progress," I said. "It's just...I'm not sure I can."

Disappointment flowed from him. "It's your first festival," he said. "Is there anything I can do to help so you can join in? Is D going to be free?"

I didn't know the answer—and I was disappointed too. "I need you to be ready to act," I said. "I don't think it'll be that fast, but if we figure it out, you and D can both show me the best way to end the festival."

"You've done great work taking the hexes down," he said. "Mrs. V told me to look out for someone falling ill. I assume it's not just the usual overexertion?"

I guessed I'd left Mark out of the hex work so he could do his job. But he would be a good set of eyes and ears in the crowd, and I couldn't watch everyone by myself.

"We've released all but five of the hexes. We need to figure out who the remaining witches are. That's what D and the others are working on right now. I needed a break, so I'm checking for sick witches." I looked around to see if anyone was a walking sick ward, but no such luck. "The only one I know about is Phillip, but he's been sick for a week, so I guess it's not him."

"Excuse me," a tall man interrupted us politely. He was tall and thin, wearing a gray cowboy hat, jeans, and a Calgary Stampede T-shirt. "I'm sorry to bother you, but I have one of your talisman blanks and I heard there might be a problem. Name's Gregory Schwartzman, by the way."

Mark held out his hand. "No problem. I'm Mark, the local cop, and this is Cossi. Let me check the talisman."

Gregory handed the wooden oval to Mark and nodded to me. "I heard you're one of the lost ones."

"Lost ones?" I asked. That described me a bit, but no one here had called me that.

He blushed. "Sorry, local jargon. Very few families have left our community over the years. Lost ones. You grew up like a plain?"

"I did. I'm happy to be here now, though. I hope I haven't messed up the talismans."

Mark handed me the blank. "What do you feel?"

I'd tested these so many times I didn't expect to feel anything. At first, I didn't. But Gregory said there was something there. So I went deeper.

A gray mist of disruption greeted me. I dropped the slice of wood.

"That wasn't there before," I said. "Phillip tested them earlier and found nothing."

"When did you get yours?" Mark asked.

"The first day. Thought it was a good souvenir. Been feeling a bit off this last day. Maybe it wasn't there to start?"

Someone had used my giveaways to make people ill? I couldn't think for a moment—or even breathe. Panic wasn't going to help. I remembered my centering exercise and got control of my... anger? Despair? Both?

"Who else has touched this?" Mark asked. "Since you received it?"

"No one as far as I know," Gregory said. "I've carried it in my pocket. Anyone could have brushed by me and cast a disruption. The bookstore was busy—maybe there?"

I looked under the counter and was surprised to see I still had a couple of blanks in the bowl. "Mark, can you test these?" I handed them to him.

He took them in his right hand, pulled a sachet out of his backpack, and sprinkled a blue powder on the wood. "They're fine," he said. "This powder turns green if there's magic present."

Like testing for a roofie in a drink.

"Take one of the clean ones," I said to Gregory. "Mark will need to hold onto your original one."

Gregory poked the talisman blanks around and then

selected one. He looked at me and reached into his pocket. "I got a feeling about you," he said. "You're going to be someone important." He handed me a pen. "I'd appreciate it if you signed it for me."

That was embarrassing, but Mark nodded when I looked at him. I smiled and carefully signed the blank on the back. "Enjoy the rest of the festival."

Mark slid the contaminated blank into an evidence bag. "I'll drop this off at the lab." We both laughed when he said it, because Mrs. V was our lab. "Be careful—and let's get those hexes canceled soon."

I wished it were that simple. We could remove the rest of those evil spells without identifying the targets, but then we'd have no idea what the link was between the victims. And, like Jeffery said, we could lose our opportunity to question the witch. Working on our assumption that it was about leveraging the influence of the leaders didn't help with five outstanding hexes.

And if someone was trying to frame me for casting bad magic... was it part of the same plot? If the answer was yes, then were we close enough to finding the truth that the hexing witch was starting to get scared?

29

I took the remaining flyers and talisman blanks with me as I hurried to check on Phillip. By now, he should be recovering a little. Whatever this illness was, no one else had shown symptoms, and Doc Rene seemed confident he was the only one suffering. The last thing we needed was a pandemic with the CDC tracking patient zero to Henbane Island.

The bookstore was closed—a pity for the people who wanted to buy something while they were here—but it meant Phillip wasn't pushing himself and weakening his system further. It occurred to me that he might be under the influence of the hexes, but his symbol was a cat's paw, and none of the unidentified images looked anything like that.

I opened the door to the apartment quietly, just in case he was resting. The place felt empty, but that was probably because he was asleep. My powers didn't extend to sensing life forces or heat signatures. They did extend to a creepy feeling of doom. Ugh. I needed time to understand all these emotions. Who knew there were so many shades of everything?

"You are a superior being," Destroyer said into my brain. "That is because I am your familiar. Most humans don't see as deeply. You are welcome for my influence."

He did make me feel a little better—not great, but not awful either. "Thank you. I guess it's also my power, but having an all-powerful emperor crow is indeed an asset."

He didn't seem to notice the sarcasm.

I put the booth contents in my room and grimaced at the mess I'd left that morning. I'm not the kind of person to make my bed every day—I have way more important things to do with my time—but this was a slob too far. My last few days' worth of clothes were in piles by the door where I'd just dropped them before crawling into bed. Research books were scattered across the side of the bed, and three teacups sat waiting to go moldy on my night table. Good thing the protection spell wouldn't let anyone into the room. Although it was going to start smelling soon.

I left Phillip to his rest while I tidied up. Clothes into the hamper, books and notepaper piled on the night table, cups stacked for washing. I made sure nothing was hiding in the folds of the duvet before I shook it out and let it fall more or less straight across the bed. Much better.

I opened the window to let some air in, then took the dishes to the kitchen. In a matter of minutes, the cups were cleaned, dried, and back in the cupboard. I hate housework, but had to admit to myself—and only myself—that mundane tasks kind of settled my mind.

I put the kettle on and went to Phillip's bedroom door. Not something I'd done in all the time I'd lived here. We kept our lives separate, even before Mrs. V took over my mentorship. But he was sick, and I'd never forgive myself if he got worse because I didn't check on him.

I knocked and waited. Nothing.

I knocked a little harder and called his name. Still nothing.

I checked the handle. Not locked.

I peeked inside. No Phillip.

Interesting. He must be feeling better if he'd gone out rather than opened the store.

The kettle whistled, and I went back to turn off the heat. I didn't need tea.

There were two more rooms to check: the bedroom Martin had used when he stayed here before his murder, and the living room. The bathroom door was open, so I knew he hadn't drowned.

Martin's room was now back to being Phillip's office. I knocked and opened the door. No one inside.

The living room was tidy, and the fireplace cleaned out. Relief flooded my body. I hadn't realized how afraid I was of finding him dead. These murders were taking my mind in a dark direction.

I hadn't heard from anyone about the remaining stones, so I headed back to the festival. Maybe wandering through the crowd would give me a clue.

30

Now I was at a loss for what to do. My booth was effectively closed, and the festivities would start in about an hour. I still needed to fulfill my original task: locate witches who fell sick today.

I shut the apartment, headed down to the street, checked in with Destroyer, and made my way toward the sound of music starting up.

My familiar was on the other side of the island when he answered me. "Taking more risks with our lives?" he asked. It sounded like an accusation in my head. "I have not heard of any witches suddenly becoming ill. I can have my army look as they attend the party. I look forward to the day when we are not at war with evil witches."

There was that drama again. "I thought your forces would be hiding," I said. "All those witches and shifters. All that noise." As I spoke, the music ramped up: guitars, drums, and bagpipes.

"There will be food dropped for scavenging. Do you need me to attend you?"

There were all kinds of reasons to say yes, and a lot of

other reasons to say no. I wouldn't be as agile with him on my shoulder—that seemed like the strongest reason to let him stay away.

"I do have emperor tasks," he said, reading my mind. "If any of my soldiers find a suspicious witch, they will report to you."

That would be enough help. The small animals had been a huge help in the past. And I could go back to Mrs. V when I was ready, without leaving the crowd unattended.

"Tomorrow, all will rest," he said. "The visitors will leave. We will be back to normal. And we can start to investigate what is happening to your power."

Something was going on with one of my powers? He wouldn't respond when I asked what he meant. It wasn't a surprise, and I'd bet a body part it was my third, dangerous power.

I continued toward the festival, tossing questions and fears around in my head. I tried to shut out the worries, but nothing worked.

My stomach growled. Was that why I couldn't get my thoughts under control? I glanced around. The food tent was busy, but the line moved fast.

Today it was a joint effort with Jan, Zoe, and Sheena. I grabbed a beer from Sheena and a bag of fries from Jan. Zoe's offerings looked and smelled fabulous, but they were the kind of thing that needed a table, chair, and napkins. I didn't want to delay my circuit of the crowd too long. I held the bag and the beer in my right hand, picked out fries with my left, then transferred the bag to take a drink. Yes, it was a bit awkward, but you do what you have to.

I started by circling the edge of the crowd. I waved to Valerie and the Barks, then spotted Mark across from me. He was talking to Gregory from earlier. Fingers crossed they'd found the source of the disruption, so I didn't have to ask Phillip if he knew what happened and risk making him think he was a suspect.

Lilibeth was standing outside the medical tent talking to Doc Rene. The tent looked empty from where I stood, so no shortcut to finding a sick witch. I made my way toward them, hoping someone had gone home after checking in. Although, as I thought of it, would the hex caster know why they were ill? If yes, there was no way they'd risk letting a healer near them.

I finished my fries and dropped the bag in a compost bin on my way to the tent. As I turned away, Phillip caught my attention. He was on the edge of the crowd across from me, leaning on a cane, talking to a shifter I didn't recognize. I didn't know many of them, so that didn't ring any alarms.

"Cossi," Buddleia Twotrees called my name. "Do you have a moment?"

It would be rude to say I was busy when I couldn't say what I was doing. So I met her near the closest path out of the party grounds.

"I hope you're enjoying the festival," I said.

"Oh, I am. I just wanted to ask you about those talisman blanks."

Oh no. What now?

"I don't have many left," I said. "But if there's a problem, I might be able to replace yours."

"Exactly the opposite, dear." She leaned in like we were sharing a secret. "I was wondering if you would be interested in making more and selling them to me?"

"I'd be happy to. How many?" I had no idea what the price should be, and I'd have to triple-check there was no unwanted magic before I shipped them.

"Two hundred," she said, hope bubbling up in a pale-yellow fountain. "Not today, of course, but within the month?"

I had the raw material for far more than her order, but I didn't have the time. A little twitch in my gut pushed me to ask why. I mean, I didn't know her—and with all the problems on the mainland with plain humans, perhaps having Henbane products all over the place wasn't a good idea.

"Two reasons," she said. "I have three nieces who would love one each, and I think I can spell them to order. So I could sell them as talismans in my store."

"There's enough market in Kincolith?" All I knew about her home was that it sat just under Alaska.

"Online store, dear." She patted my arm. "I'd be happy to do a split with you rather than pay up front. Say twenty percent?"

I knew I should think it over, but I had more important things on my mind. The offer was fair since I wasn't doing any of the spell work.

"Can you email me the details to The Inner Spell address? You have that, right?"

She nodded. "Two hundred blanks, within the month. You ship them, and I pay you twenty percent commission. You'll sign them, of course. People will want to know the provenance."

That sounded a bit over the top. I thought the word was only used for famous art pieces. "Perfect. Just for the two hundred," I said. "If it's successful, we'll work something more permanent out."

She patted my arm again and walked away, already typing on her phone.

While that was a great business opportunity, it had taken me away from my mission. I glanced around—and Phillip was nowhere to be seen.

31

"Hey, I thought I wouldn't see you until it was all over." Lilibeth bumped my arm. "It would be a pity for you to miss the party."

I guessed she was on a break, and I wanted to hear all the stories about the festival she had to share—but I needed her help to find Phillip. We'd have plenty of time to gossip once the latest crisis was over.

"We've had a bit of a breakthrough," I said. "The whole hex thing could be over soon."

"I heard from Mark. He and D told us what's going on. Great news on the progress! Are you on a hunt for the remaining witches? Can I help?"

Help would be great.

"I need to find Phillip." I updated her on the problem with the talisman blanks. "I want to ask if he felt anything like that when he tested one earlier." And keep looking for witches suffering from hex bounce-back. I kept that part to myself.

"I saw him around. He's not looking fit, but if he's here,

he must be feeling better than he looks." She scanned the crowd. "There he is."

She pointed to a group of witches—I recognized most of them as earth witches. And Phillip was resting just behind them.

"Let's go," Lilibeth said. She grabbed my arm and led me around the edge of the crowd. "Before he decides to go home. You can ask him and then we can grab a beer. Maybe Lance and D will be able to join us."

I'd rather D stayed away. His work with Jeffery was more important. I did like having Lilibeth with me. I'm not sure why. I mean, I could find Phillip and ask him a few innocent questions without her help, but it just felt better not to be alone. A warm glow settled in my gut again as we worked our way toward him.

"Who's that?" Lilibeth asked.

I glanced up from the ground. I'd been looking down to make sure I didn't stumble over someone sitting outside the tight clump of attendees.

"Gregory Schwartzman," I said, recognizing the witch from Calgary. "He took one of the last blanks. I didn't know he and Phillip were friends."

"I'm not sure they are," Lilibeth said.

She had a point—the conversation didn't seem all that friendly. Phillip was glaring up at Gregory, who was bent down almost in Phillip's face. A few steps more, and I saw the emotions, ugly bruise colors, floating above them.

A moment later we were close enough to hear a few words.

"Are you still bullying people?" Gregory hissed at Phillip.

"I don't know what you're talking about," Phillip said, putting his hands up as though he were going to push the other witch away.

No one else seemed to hear their exchange—or they were doing a good job of ignoring them.

"Phillip a bully?" Lilibeth whispered, pulling me to a stop.

"He's a bit spiteful," I said, remembering his behavior when Mrs. V took over my mentorship. "Bully? I don't know."

"You've changed, Phillip Raziel," Gregory said. "A lot. I'm not sure I believe it. But you have the protector here, and she's not easy to fool."

"Sir, I have never met you in my life," Phillip said. He used his cane to push himself upright, forcing Gregory to step back. "What lies have you been told?"

"I've grown a lot," Gregory said. "My parents took me away to stop you from terrorizing me. It's no surprise you don't recall me. Now. I'm too big for you to push around."

What the heck?

Lilibeth and I stood there, dumbfounded. Our shock twisted together to form a tangerine umbrella of protection. Another new thing? I really needed time to understand these changes in my power.

Gregory stomped off, not noticing us—or not caring who saw him.

Phillip turned away and limped into the trees surrounding the festival grounds. I couldn't make my voice work to call out to him.

Suddenly, it didn't matter about the talismans.

32

"It must be a mistake," Lilibeth said. "Phillip is a council member. He's well respected. He took oaths."

Were witches so different? In my past life, being a bully didn't bar you from leadership roles. In fact, a bit of aggressiveness was considered an asset.

"It was a long time ago," I said. "Even if it's not a mistake. Gregory said his parents took him away from the island, and he must be what? A hundred?"

"Phillip's age for sure," Lilibeth said. "Yeah, maybe when they were kids. Maybe Phillip was a bully. But he grew out of it? Or his parents turned him to a new path?"

"I need to get back to Mrs. V," I said. "Can you let me know if someone gets suddenly ill? The hexes should be snapping back to the caster by now."

"No one yet," she said. "Lots of normal 'I'm too busy having fun to think about heat or dehydration' stuff. I'll text you if anything unusual turns up."

I gave her a hug before racing back to Mrs. V. This news about Phillip was too important to just walk.

. . .

"I REMEMBER THE SCHWARTZES," Mrs. V said when I shared the news with her, Jeffery, and D. "Left early on. No one knew exactly why and didn't ask. If people wanted to risk being among the plain humans, then they were welcome to do it."

"They were older than me," Jeffery said. "Phillip was out of school when I started, so I didn't know much about him. Bullies are hard to deal with. Some kids just come out mean and there's no shaping their path."

I thought about the reasons kids on the mainland turned into bullies. Hard home life. A need to feel in control of something—even if it was a scared, smaller kid. It didn't sound like that was true on Henbane. And it wasn't the time to debate nature versus nurture.

"Could it be a mistake?" I asked, because that was Lilibeth's first reaction.

"Unlikely," Mrs. V said. "Phillip looked pretty much the same as a child."

"He looked bad too," I said. "Using a cane. His voice was weak."

"Doc Rene needs to see him again," Jeffery said. "You don't know this, Cossi, but witches tend not to have lingering illness. Phillip isn't old enough to be dying."

I let it go. We could look into Phillip's past when we'd found the witch behind the hexes. "Any luck in identifying the remaining symbols?"

"Effie and Herman," Jeffery said. "The loaf of bread and the flute. I'm sure I know the others, but I'm still having problems with my memory filing system."

"We don't want to remove them all," Mrs. V said with a snap of her fingers. "It could kill the caster. I want to have a long talk with him—or her—before we apply the correct punishment. Two more removals should be safe. Do you feel up to it?"

I wasn't sure what Herman brought to the theory that it was all influential people, but setting him free didn't require a reason other than it was the right thing to do.

"Let's set it up."

We were efficient this time. Mrs. V had a protective circle ready. The two hexes were in the center of the table. Jeffery and D stood well out of range of any unexpected reactions.

I cleared my mind and dissolved the magic. The odor was the same no matter how many we released at once. This time, someone had thought ahead—the patio door slid open on a spell to circulate clean air.

Mrs. V cleared the table. "Time to go enjoy the party. We're not going to suddenly identify the remaining witches. A rest is the best way to clear and invigorate the mind."

She shooed us out.

D and I linked arms and headed for the festival grounds again. Jeffery muttered something about going home to think.

33

"What is this party like?" I asked D as we approached the edge of the festival grounds. My booth was only a row of stalls away.

"It's not all alcohol and dancing," he said. "Most of it, sure, but first we talk about hopes for next year. People exchange promises to meet and make plans for the future. The elders will cast a spell of good feeling before we start."

"So people will... I don't know, have fun? Isn't that kind of coercive?"

He laughed at the idea. "No, it's so people will be serious about their intentions. Everyone who's here has to agree for the spell to work, so no one's forced to do anything."

Because only I could bind people to an agreement without them knowing. Maybe I could use my third power as some kind of magical notary. Plenty of time to think about that in a couple of days. By then, we'd have the whole hex thing worked out and Mrs. V would tell the council I had a banned power.

I didn't feel the usual touch of dread at the thought of losing it. I guessed I'd think about that later too.

"Isn't that your booth?" D asked, pulling me to the side.

It was—and I saw what had caught his attention. The side curtains were gaping open and hanging crooked, like someone had grabbed them to halt a fall.

"Maybe I can fix it," I said, unhooking my arm from his. My gut was tingling again. I had no idea what to make of the potential intuition. "It looks sloppy. I don't want people thinking I can't keep a booth in one piece."

We got closer, and suddenly my steps felt like I was moving through honey.

"What is that?" I asked D. Then I noticed he was struggling too.

"A warding spell," he said. "Something's wrong. Let me call Mark before we stumble onto something."

I waited while D sent a text.

"He'll be here in a few minutes," D read from his phone. "Wants us to keep quiet about whatever it is."

I agreed. No need to spoil the party if we didn't have to.

As promised, Mark showed up with Roy in tow.

"Not good," Roy said in my mind.

"When was the last time you were here?" Mark asked. "Just in case we need to set a timeline."

"An hour ago, maybe a little more," I said, sifting through my memory. "Nothing was wrong then. Maybe someone stumbled and used the curtain to stay upright?"

"Maybe," Mark said, doubt swirling around him. "Is there a closing spell on it right now?"

"Yes." I offered to release it, but Mark reminded me he could break any lock.

"It's probably nothing, but best to be safe," he said.

"I'd agree," D added, "except for the warding spell. Why cast that if it was an accident? It's not like anyone's going to charge them for the damage. And no one would go in there anyway."

Mark thought it over. Normally he would have just acted, but since we'd broken the controlling spell someone had placed on him, he was a bit hesitant now. I hoped he'd get over that soon. It was kind of irritating, even though I understood his fear that everything he knew had changed.

He turned to his police dog. "Roy, anything to be worried about?"

He couldn't hear what Roy said, but I could. I translated the barks into human. "There's pepper," I said. "Roy can smell something is wrong, but not exactly what. You shouldn't go in alone."

The last part was from me.

"I'll be okay. But maybe you can both watch from the front? In case you need to go for help."

As in Doc Rene—or a council member.

We followed him around to the front of the booth. Roy waited at Mark's side while he removed the ward, and the closing spell I'd cast.

Roy stuck his nose inside before Mark could move. He growled and backed out.

Mark looked inside. I peeked over his shoulder.

Gregory Schwartzman was lying on his back in the middle of the booth, a talisman blank in one hand and a scrap of paper in the other.

Please just be passed out.

Mark checked for a pulse. "We're too late," he said.

34

"I'll get Doc Rene," D said. "Just in case. And if he's dead, we need to know when and how, right?"

Mark nodded and held out a hand to stop me from moving forward. I hoped it wasn't because he didn't want me to help with his investigation. I thought we were past that, given everything my friends and I had done in the last few cases. But if I was right, and he was still feeling a bit shaken by the release of that spell, he might want to work on his own. We'd run separate investigations in the past, so it wasn't a deal breaker. That twitch in my gut happened again—like it was telling me to tread carefully. Not to let Mark do his job, but to be careful not to stomp all over him in my haste to fix things.

For a second, I wondered if there was a possibility I had four powers, and one of them existed just to keep me from making things worse.

"No one goes in until Doc Rene has a chance to look."

Well, that wasn't a stay away from the case, but it also wasn't an invitation to join the team.

"How do you know him?" Mark asked.

"What makes you think I..." I said, then sighed. "Okay, yes. I met him. He's from Calgary. His name is Gregory Schwartzman. I gave him a talisman blank—probably the one he's holding."

"That's it?" Mark asked.

"And he was arguing with Phillip earlier." I filled him in on what we'd overheard.

"So, suspect number one," Mark said.

"I'm not a suspect?" I asked. I mean, he was in my booth, but that didn't mean I'd done anything.

"We'll see," he said with a laugh. "I'm pretty sure you have an alibi. Between him being alive, yelling at Phillip, and now, you've been with Mrs. V, right?"

"Yes, but how did you know?" *Did he have a tracker on me?*

"I know everything," he said, narrowing his eyes at me.

We both laughed—until we remembered the dead body.

"Jeffery mentioned you'd released more hexes," Mark said.

"Okay, I'm here," Doc Rene stepped between us. "Oh dear, this is going to put a damper on things."

"Not yet," Mark said. "I'd like to keep this between us until we have to announce it. Let people enjoy the night."

Doc Rene stepped inside, pulling on a pair of latex gloves. "Definitely dead," she said as she checked for a pulse or any reflex. "Help me turn him," she said to us. "And keep Roy out for now, please."

Roy sat as if on guard. Mark and I carefully turned Gregory onto his belly. Cause of death seemed quite clear—a nasty bash to the back of his head.

"Roll him back," Doc Rene said. "That's not enough to kill. Definitely life-changing if he survived, but not fatal."

I wasn't sure I believed her, but we turned him back. Then I realized D was absent.

"Where is D?"

"I sent him to tell Dolph and Mrs. V," Doc Rene said. "We need them to cooperate if you want to keep this quiet. And that's best done in person."

At least I wouldn't have to inform them. I'd take one small mercy from this awful situation. I watched as Doc Rene bent close to Gregory's mouth. She sniffed and then applied a little pressure to his chest.

"Nutmeg," Doc Rene pronounced. "Poison. Maybe the combination of the injury and Myristica oil killed him. I need someone to bring him to the clinic."

"It should be easy to take him out back without anyone noticing," I said. "Everyone is around the stage."

Mark looked up from his phone. "Dolph is sending two shifters. And Lance, to help us."

"Who was he staying with?" I asked. "Won't they worry that something's wrong?"

"Azalea," Doc Rene said. "I saw them together earlier. She'll think he's partying. If you can't solve this quick, we'll have to tell her."

The circle of insiders was getting pretty large.

35

M rs. V showed up just as I started to worry about the news getting out accidentally.

"You think this is related?" she asked Mark. "To the other deaths? It could be a coincidence, yes?"

Mark looked at me like I had the answer. I mean, I hadn't really considered it being just a murder—something unrelated to whoever we were hunting.

"We won't know until we solve it," he said. "I'm sorry I can't say anything more hopeful."

"Don't be an idiot," she snapped, a wave of purple annoyance practically rolling off her. "If this is part of the bigger plot, we're closer to solving the case. If it's a separate crime altogether, then it's a distraction. I'm sorry to say it, but this witch's death is the most untimely one ever."

I was sure Gregory hadn't planned to be killed, but I understood what she meant. We thought we were finally on the brink of making an arrest—just not of Gregory's killer. Now we had to drop everything and solve a murder.

The shifters arrived with a hand-pushed cart—kind of like a wheelbarrow, but longer and more square. We stepped aside as Doc Rene directed them to load the body and cover it with a light blanket.

"I'll meet you at the clinic," she said. "Lilibeth will handle the crowd and whatever happens for the rest of the party. She'll join me once things settle down. I'll let you know as soon as I have news."

With that, she trotted after the body movers and left us standing there. There wasn't much more to do than scan the area while we waited for Lance to arrive—and maybe D, once he'd finished his round of notifications.

"Who are your suspects?" Mrs. V asked, looking at both Mark and me.

"We only have Phillip right now," I said. "It's not much, but he did argue with the victim. And I guess Azalea—since Gregory was her guest."

"And any of the off-island witches who might have known him," she added. "If this is linked, we may have another witch being used as a weapon."

Guessing our way through a growing list of suspects wouldn't help. If we wanted to keep this quiet until we found the killer, we couldn't go around randomly interviewing anyone who might've crossed paths with Gregory.

"I'll ask Destroyer if any animals saw anything," I said. "And I might be able to sense guilt—like I did in the crowd earlier." I couldn't mention the other power without getting myself into trouble. But Mrs. V knew I'd use it if I had to.

"What if the killer doesn't feel guilty?" Mark asked. "What if they think it was justified? Would you still pick up on that? It would be great if your magic worked to filter out suspects."

"We'll see what happens." Mrs. V tipped her chin toward the far side of the booth curtains. I followed her out.

"We'll go to that end of the grounds," she said, pointing

to a small rise next to the stage. "Test your perceptions. Look for guilt, yes, but also for a level of satisfaction that doesn't quite fit. What else?"

"I haven't done much to classify what I feel from people," I admitted. "I just know it when I see it—or smell it."

She pursed her lips, thoughtfully. "So your other senses are involved? Interesting. Let's see what you can find. Not everyone is here, so it might not prove anything."

"Who isn't in the crowd?" I asked, following her up to the vantage point, trying not to trip as Destroyer flooded me with reports. Apparently, Gregory had been easy to spot and generous with animal snacks.

"Destroyer says no one saw the murder, but he'll get them to look for clues," I said, then sent a quick text to Mark: Look out for a swarm of searchers.

He replied with a thumbs-up emoji.

"There are a few witches who needed to rest," Mrs. V said, finally answering my question. "Not all of us are young enough to party all night."

"I guess that would make them too frail to kill a witch in his prime," I said, and waited for the reaction. Mrs. V hated being thought of as frail.

"Yes. Even with poison, it would take some strength. We should think about why he went into your booth—with someone who was planning to kill."

36

I looked out over the crowd and took in the whole stew of emotions.

"Tell me what you see," Mrs. V said, giving me a gentle—ish—nudge.

"Mostly people are excited," I said. "A few probably too tired to be here but sticking it out. I guess that's determination?"

"You're developing a keen sense," she said. "Many would not call that an emotion."

I took the praise and scanned deeper. "Really low levels of annoyance, but it's because they're tired and little things are getting on their nerves. Someone over in the earth witch crowd just had a burst of inspiration."

"So our killer isn't here," Mrs. V said scanning the area. "Unless... is there a void of emotion?"

"No. I thought of that right away. A psychopath wouldn't feel anything, right?"

"Interesting," Mrs. V murmured again.

I followed her gaze and saw Elias, the island contractor, sitting with a few shifters. When he worked on The Inner

Spell, I hadn't sensed any emotion from him. Now, there was a faint stirring of curiosity.

"Yes, he's feeling something," I said. "Maybe not much, but definitely more than before."

"One of the hexes was a hammer," she said. "Perhaps..."

"You think we weakened the hexes on everyone as we released them?"

"If that's Elias's symbol, it's possible. I don't think anyone considered a hex—we just blamed the accident."

I had no idea what the real story was with Elias and his lack of emotions. But if we'd done something to bring them back, I'd be happy to take the win.

"We should go back," I said. "The small animals might've found something." I hesitated, a new idea forming from this test of my powers. "What about my third power? If I used it on the suspects... would that be an abuse?"

She ushered me toward the booths. "You think you can persuade the killer to confess?"

"I'm worried it would force a false confession," I said. The problem with a coercive power was you never knew if the result was the truth—or just the truth you wanted. That's why the council would probably end up ordering me to suppress it again.

"I don't know," Mrs. V said. She pulled me to the side of the first booth. No one was around, so we could talk. "It would help speed things up, but it would also expose your power. Is it worth the risk?"

To find the killer? Especially if it was the person behind all the murders?

Yes.

"I'm willing to chance it," I said. "This is such a threat to Henbane—I couldn't live with myself if I didn't use it. Even if it means I'll have to drink licorice tea for the rest of my life to squash it."

She kept her gaze locked on mine. I couldn't look away, though I desperately wanted to.

"Try to make me confess." She narrowed her eyes, like a shield braced against my power.

What the heck?

"Will it work if you know what I'm doing?" I asked.

"This power has nothing to do with my intent—only yours."

I wished the impulse toward her the way I imagined I'd do it with a real suspect: Confess to what you did to Gregory Schwartzman, the witch from Calgary.

"I most certainly did nothing," she said. "I felt a seeking when you used it. And something more. We'll explore it— once our work is done here."

37

Mrs. V left me to go back to her house and, I figured, do more research. If it were up to me, I'd release the remaining hexes first and then get around to finding who cast them—and who killed Gregory. But I was still too new to this whole being-a-witch thing to have full faith in what I thought was best.

A little voice inside my head shouted, *You are right*. I ignored it.

Time to do some investigating and leave the big picture planning to Mrs. V. I stepped into the alley between booths to check if the animals had found any clues.

"Where should we start?" D asked, falling into step beside me. "It's weird, right? We don't seem to get any better at this investigating thing, no matter how many we solve."

I hoped we wouldn't get the opportunity to practice more.

"Let's check in with Mark. Maybe he has an assignment for us."

When we got to my booth, Mark was surrounded by mice and squirrels. He looked up and beckoned me over.

"Looks like they found a clue," he said, "but it's not something they can bring. Or maybe I've got it all wrong."

I asked the animals to choose a representative. That sparked a debate over who would get the credit. I left them to it and turned to Mark.

"Yes, they found a clue—or at least, they think it's a clue. I'll get the story in a minute."

He rubbed his forehead. "What did Mrs. V want?"

I filled him in on our lack of success—but not on the decision to use my third power during interrogation.

"Where's Lance? Didn't Dolph tell him to help?"

"I sent him to check on the witches who aren't here," Mark said. "All the shifters are present, as far as I can tell. Dolph can confirm that if we need him to."

"We are ready," a tiny mouse interrupted.

I gave him the signal to report.

"You saw this thing," he said, pushing a talisman blank toward me with his nose.

"Yes, but that's one I gave him," I said.

"There is no magic on that one," he said. "Found near where dead witch was."

If that was the extent of his help, I really needed to work on some training with Destroyer's army.

"It is not all," he said. I hadn't spoken aloud, so that was a bit disconcerting.

"What else?" I asked, then apologized for jumping the gun.

He looked over his shoulder, and two squirrels marched forward with two more talismans and a handful of my flyers. My remaining supply was in my bedroom. It was disappointing to realize witches were discarding the information almost as soon as they took it.

"Where did you find these?" Mark asked.

I translated, then waited while the squirrels and mouse discussed the answer.

"What's taking them so long?" D asked. "Are they making up a lie?"

I shook my head. So far, the animals hadn't been able to lie to me. "I think they're trying to translate the distance into something other than three thousand mouse steps."

"Yes," Destroyer said in my mind. "It is not far."

Nice to have my guess confirmed. Of course, not far to a crow was as likely to be too far to humans and really far to a mouse could be around the corner.

"We can't agree on a distance," the mouse said. "We show you."

"Before we leave, did you find other clues?" Small animals often got sidetracked, so I wasn't going to risk missing anything by not asking.

"Three legs," the mouse said. "Went from here. Too shallow for witches to see. We go now."

He hopped impatiently.

"Should we all go?" I asked Mark. "These guys think it's important, but I don't think we should leave the site unprotected."

Mark cast a locking spell around my booth and nodded. "Lead the way."

38

After a few minutes, we were standing in a small clearing in the woods. In the center was a pile of ash.

Mark walked over and held his hand above the remnants of the fire. "Still some warmth."

"Here is where three legs came. Burned papers and seeds. Say your name," the squirrel told me, his head tilted. "Why?"

I had no idea, and I told him so. "Thank you for your help."

He jumped in excitement and led the squirrels off toward the nearest food box.

"Good thing you have a solid alibi," Mark said. "This is a spell meant to direct my investigation to you."

I swallowed the sudden rise of fear in my throat. "Why isn't it working on you?"

"Because he has your alibi," D said, giving me a hug. "But for people who don't know, it'll build suspicion."

"I'll disable it," Mark said. "Let's hope no one's been affected yet."

I watched as he tossed a handful of green powder into the pit and stirred it with a gesture.

"You should talk to some of the residents," Mark said when he finished. "Find out if anyone remembers Phillip being different—back when he was a kid. I have a really bad feeling about this. Is anyone else using a cane?"

I thought back over the last few days. "I haven't seen anyone but him with one. That doesn't mean he did this. I've mostly been in my booth and at Mrs. V's. I haven't seen a lot of people." I didn't need to ask what his bad feeling was—he thought Phillip killed Gregory.

"There are a couple of witches with canes," D said, clearly on the same wavelength. "It can't be Phillip, right?"

"It can," Mark said, rubbing his head again. "Just because we don't want it to be him doesn't mean it isn't. Too many things are piling up against him. He's been ill. He's using a cane. I'll go look for the other witches who use one. You both talk to enough people to get a handle on Phillip's past—in case the hexes affected everyone's memory. We can't just arrest him with this little evidence. He's a council member. He took an oath. If it is Phillip, we have a much bigger problem."

We split up—Mark placing a call to Lance to get information on cane-using witches, while D and I headed back into the crowd.

"Who should we talk to?" I asked.

"Valerie. Anyone sitting with her. Zoe, if she's not with them. Maybe the Barks? They were all under the hex until you cleared it. After that?" D shrugged. "It's going to depend on what we learn."

39

Valerie was sitting by herself at the edge of the crowd. "I like to be able to slip out if I get too tired," she said as we approached.

D told her what I'd heard the victim say to Phillip—not that he used the word victim—and she looked surprised.

"I should remember him clearly," she said. "It was a long time ago, even for a witch. He was in school with only twenty people, if I remember correctly. We had two decades when few births happened, so it was a range of ages in one class."

"Was Phillip a difficult kid?" I asked, trying to steer her back to the question.

She frowned, as though digging for more than just a vague feeling. After a few moments, she shook her head, frustration rising from her body.

"I don't recall. No details at all from around that time. You'd think I could bring up something—a graduation, a prank—but no. All I sense is that Phillip and the other children were happy and curious. Hmm. Perhaps I'm getting older than my years."

It was odd. She'd remembered plenty about my parents, and they were around the same age as Phillip—at least, I thought so.

"Thanks for giving us what you remember," I said. "I guess I was worried Gregory might stain Phillip's reputation."

We said goodbye just as the shifters took the stage and announced the music would start in ten minutes.

"The Barks are over there," D said, pointing to the far edge of the crowd. "A lot of the older witches seem to plan a quick exit."

Along with Alder and Violet Bark sat Zoe, the proprietor of Food For Us. She was tiny and had a wicked sense of humor, as I'd discovered during my first meal in her café.

"Odd," Alder Bark said after we asked about Phillip as a child. "There's something of a blank space in those years. I'll do a seeking if it's important."

"We'll let you know," D said. "You should enjoy the party."

"I did some teaching at the school when Phillip was there," Zoe said. "My memory is perfectly fine. I can give you details, but... the kids from those years were particularly pleasant and eager to learn." She frowned. "Now that I say it aloud, it sounds ridiculous."

The bagpipes started up.

"I think it's helpful," I said over the noise. "I hope you have fun tonight."

We walked away from the stage to a slightly quieter area.

"They all remember it differently," I said. "But no one thinks Phillip was a problem child."

"Zoe is suspicious of her memory," D said. "If it's the hexes, the spell is wearing down—slowly."

"I still can't believe Phillip would kill. I mean, yes, maybe there's a hex on him, but wouldn't his oath override it?"

"We'll find out, Cossi. I don't think anyone is going to like what's about to happen," D said. "I'll text my parents to confirm, but as far as I can tell, someone's manipulated their memories."

"And we only have one person who'd benefit," I said. "Despite what we think, Phillip has moved up the suspect list."

40

My phone buzzed before I could even start coming up with reasons Phillip was innocent —the man who offered me a home when I was alone, about to be evicted, and stunned by the fact that my whole life up to then had been a lie.

"Mrs. V," I said, looking over at D, who was also checking a text.

"We've both been summoned," he said. "Maybe she's found some clues?"

We'd have been headed there anyway with the new information. Maybe she'd have a reason Phillip couldn't be the killer, the one behind all the problems.

It only took a few minutes to reach her cottage—without stopping for my usual treats. None of the animals interrupted us. Destroyer told me to focus on my job when I checked in with him. Good thing D was with me, or I'd have felt decidedly alone.

"Interesting," Mrs. V said when I finished updating her on the afternoon's events. "And it may be the first step in finally reading Martin Light's diary."

The book was open on the table beside a sheet of paper filled with her writing and doodles.

She pointed to a series of... words was probably the best description. But they shifted as you looked at them, sometimes turning into numbers. Definitely something new.

"I've been thinking about Martin," Mrs. V said. "He wouldn't have used any modern technology. I think that's why you haven't had success, Didier. But now that you tell me Phillip Raziel is a real suspect, I'm certain you were right —and that his name appears several times in the earlier parts of the journal."

"Maybe I can use modern tech to speed up the translation." D pulled out his laptop. "If you're right, and Martin didn't use a complicated code, I can feed the symbols in here with Phillip's name as the key and let the program do the sorting."

I crossed my fingers—not caring whether it would bring good luck or bad. We needed answers.

"Why would Martin stay with Phillip?" I asked while we waited. "If the book confirms what we think, he'd be more likely to avoid him."

"A very good question," Mrs. V said. "Perhaps the answer is in the diary." She stared at the screen as the program worked.

It wasn't like TV, where the screen fills with rotating letters and cryptic codes. That would have at least been interesting. Instead, we got the twirling circle of patience and a blank page—the most boring wait signal since on-hold music.

Then the screen blinked. And the page was full of words —ones we could read.

Phillip Raziel is not to be trusted.

41

T he very first line of the diary—written eighty years ago—contained the information we needed.

Mrs. V grasped my wrist and held me in place. The pain from her grip snapped me out of my shock. I was standing, staring at the screen. When had I moved from the chair?

"Slow down," she said. "He's not going anywhere. We need to read what we can to make sure this is proof—not just resentment or some other petty grudge."

My thoughts scattered, racing in all directions, each one demanding attention.

"Stop!" Destroyer yelled through the chaos. "You are making me dizzy. I cannot help if I fall from the sky."

Of course. The animals could find Phillip if he wasn't at home. Now that I had a little control again, things started to click into place.

Phillip was sick—and it started around the time we freed Mark. He wasn't getting better. In fact, he was getting worse. He'd illegally suppressed my coercion power. And every time we released hexes, he declined even more. How had I missed that?

"I think you were wise to keep the spell bag Mark made for you," D said, scanning the pages. "Your magic must have been looking out for you from the start."

"How were we so blind to the clues?" I asked. "How could everyone have fallen for it?"

"It would be a small matter to keep misdirecting our thoughts," D said, flipping to the next page.

I was reading the words, but nothing was sinking in.

"But now we're able to see the truth?" I asked—then realized the answer. "He's weakened. The spell is losing effectiveness."

"That, and the spell cannot obscure this much evidence," Mrs. V said. "Can you print this out?"

"Sure. Enough for each of the council members—or one fewer than usual, I guess."

"The council will need this proof," she said. "Eventually, the residents must be told. I'd prefer the visitors to be gone before this becomes public. Phillip has wound himself into the core of Henbane. We need to understand how he's violating his oath without consequence. People must not lose trust in us."

I hadn't even thought about what this revelation would mean for the island—and for the protectors.

That twinge in my gut found a voice and it has said protectors not one but lots. It wasn't the time to ask if there were other protectors. I mean, that voice couldn't just be my subconscious... could it? As far as I knew, Mrs. V was the protector, not a protector.

Why was I undermining my own belief?

"What do we do?" D asked, his voice barely above a whisper.

"Tell your parents to delay their return," Mrs. V said, all business. "If something goes wrong, we need someone ready to come to the rescue."

"And Phillip?" I asked. "We can't arrest him in secret."

"We will find him," Mrs. V said. Then she turned her head toward Tulip, who was stalking the room—her little tail high and fluffed out.

"True, my dear," she said. "Destroyer will be of great help."

"And who should be with us?" D asked. "Mark, obviously. But I think we might need reinforcements."

"First, we find him," Mrs. V said. "He is not pretending to be weak which is an advantage for us. We'll hold him while help and witnesses arrive. Dolph. Jeffery—whose memory loss, I imagine, is Phillip's doing. That will be enough. The full council will convene quickly if we need them."

I thought back to our last arrests. "Doc Rene should be there. Phillip might be the bad guy, but he is sick."

Mrs. V nodded. "Another reason to find him. I don't want him to die without explaining."

D sent a text to Lance, asking him to focus on finding Phillip. I told Destroyer to help.

"As you wish," he said, in a tone that was far from imperial.

Had he changed his mind about world domination?

"We'll go to the most obvious place," Mrs. V said. "The bookstore and your apartment. Unless, of course, your animals lead us somewhere else."

D closed his laptop after sending the print order. I heard Mrs. V's printer come creaking to life as we stepped out and closed the door behind us.

42

I t didn't take long for Destroyer's contacts to tell us where Phillip had been. Right now, that didn't matter. Hopefully, the animals could be more specific.

"Do we know where he is now?" I asked Destroyer, speaking aloud so everyone would know what was going on.

"We are trying to order the scents," Destroyer said with a sigh—who knew crows sighed?

I passed that on to D and Mrs. V. "We should wait," I added. "If Destroyer can tell us where Phillip is, we'll save a lot of time. If we run around the festival, we'll probably just miss him all night—and alert him to the search."

And then he'd slip off the island before we ever found him.

I still had my doubts, but they were eroding by the second. I figured he might be able to explain away each individual accusation—but not all of them together. Unless he really was innocent.

I thought I was a good reader of character, especially with my newly awakened powers. Sure, lots of people could mask their emotions, and I'd encountered that before. I didn't blame anyone—it's not a crime to want your reactions to remain private.

"What are you looking so pensive about?" Mrs. V asked, clearly annoyed with everything. "Has your familiar responded?"

A nice reminder that I didn't need magic to know someone's mood.

"I keep circling Phillip's guilt," I said. "I mean, there's got to be a real motive in there if we're right. But I've never felt anything from him to support our theory."

"He's blocked you," D said. "Maybe to hide his reaction to something?"

I reminded them it was easy to block me—almost everyone had done it at some point, even my three closest friends. But eventually something leaked past whatever shield they used.

"What about projecting a different emotion?" I asked. "Can that be done?"

Mrs. V left the room without a word, presumably to consult one of her research books. Or maybe just to pace off some frustration.

D sat beside me and gave me a hug. "You can't blame yourself. You barely know any of us here. How could you possibly understand people so soon?"

He meant well—but he didn't know me either. I'd been confident in my understanding of people when I thought I was just a regular human. But ever since I'd moved here and started exploring my powers, all I'd done was second-guess myself.

"I lived with him," I said. "I'll move into The Inner Spell as soon as we're done here. And I saw him get sick when we released Mark. I should have connected the dots. Even now, I'm trying to find a way to make him innocent.

It's like he's a kindly uncle with a serial killer hiding in his heart."

"He's home," Destroyer said, cutting through my downward spiral. "Stop feeling sorry for yourself and save the island."

Mrs. V returned just as he ended the connection.

"I will need to seek deeper," she said, "but I found nothing to prove or disprove the ability to project false emotions."

I let that go. Like everything else so far, it wasn't a clear answer.

"Maybe we can get Phillip to tell us," I said. No maybe about it—I was going to use my third power to make him explain, no matter the consequences to me.

We waited while Mrs. V packed a few potions and powders. Then she handed each of us a knotted rope bracelet.

"To ward off any magic he might try to use. Let's go."

I sent a text to Mark, Dolph, Lance, Jeffery, and Doc Rene: *Meet us at the bookstore apartment in twenty minutes.*

I wanted just a little time with Phillip before the room got crowded.

43

I let D and Mrs. V into the apartment through the side door. Phillip's bedroom was to the left, mine a little farther down. Our suspect was in the kitchen, a steaming mug of honey lemon tea on the table in front of him.

"I thought you'd be at the party," he said, his voice barely above a whisper. "Or out searching for our latest killer."

Mrs. V looked at him, shaking her head. "I should have known, Cossi. I've been holed up dealing with other problems. Had I seen him sooner, Gregory might still be alive."

"What are you implying?" Phillip asked, trying for affront but not having the energy to pull it off.

"Accusing you," Mrs. V said. "You cast fifteen hexes. You killed every murder victim—through others—until Gregory. This time, I believe you did the deed yourself. Only because you lost control over your victims."

"Oh, please," he said. "Why would I kill anyone? How? I'm a council member. As for the hexes, I was a child. I'd forgotten they existed. Bring them here, and I'll remove the spell."

He didn't know we'd already done that?

"Why?" I asked. "Even as a kid—why cast such an awful spell?" It had to be the motive behind everything that happened since.

"Some petty insult, I assume," Mrs. V said. "There's no need to remove the hexes. We completed that task."

"Thank you," he said, gesturing to his body. "That explains my condition. Backlash is unpleasant. But, as I said, I was a child. At that age, we don't think about consequences."

"You will answer my questions," Mrs. V said. "I am the Protector. You will have no choice."

Phillip glanced at me. "The council will not accept a compelled confession. Yes, you have that power as the Protector, but so does Cossi. I will expose her secret."

"Go ahead," I said—more confidently than I felt, now that I was about to risk everything for the truth.

44

D olph was the first council member to arrive, stepping through the door just as Phillip made his accusation.

"Perhaps we should call the entire council together," Phillip said with a bitter laugh. "Send these others away— except the new witch. She is as much at fault as I am."

Mrs. V seemed to consider his request to leave us alone. She was blocking my powers, so I had no way to sense her reasoning. I hoped she'd say no. We needed to get him to talk before going public about my third power. That was the plan—and letting Phillip derail it now was dangerous.

The fact that he was trying to blame me was ridiculous. To everyone but my inner critic.

She niggled at me with questions: If I'd chosen another community, would everyone still be alive—and under a hex?

I knew the answer to that. Phillip's actions started long before I was born, I told her. My presence just brought things to a critical point.

She sniffed in disbelief. I told her to shut her trap. Then

immediately worried I was going crazy—talking to my inner critic in the middle of a crisis.

Don't get sidetracked!

I wrangled my self-doubt into a corner and refocused—but I'd already missed Mrs. V's answer.

I didn't need to ask what it was. D and Lance slipped out. Jeffery and Dolph cast a restraining spell on Phillip. Mark moved to stand behind me. What I felt from him was pure protection.

"I'm sorry about this, Cossi," Dolph said just before casting the same spell on me. "You've both been accused. It would be wrong to only restrain Phillip."

So this was what a restraining spell felt like—nothing.

I could move around and sit with no problem, but the moment I took even half a step toward the doorway—even just to head to my room—I hit invisible jelly. Not physical, but something resisted my will. Light at first, then thicker and thicker, until I worried I wouldn't be able to breathe.

I sat at the table across from Phillip after testing the boundaries.

"I get it," I said, trying to ease Dolph's tension—and relieve Jeffery from the embarrassment tightening his jaw. "How long is this going to take? And if I need to use the bathroom, what do I do?"

Dolph grinned like he knew I was trying to lift the mood. "Let us know, and someone will escort you. The others are on their way. It shouldn't take long."

The rest of the council arrived within five minutes. All sober—but likely due to a spell, not restraint.

"The party is in full swing," Effie said. "This better be good. Why are these two restrained? What the heck is going on, Patience?"

Mrs. V—Patience—explained everything we'd uncovered and confirmed. "Phillip has pointed the finger at Cossi in an effort to buy time."

"Did you cast the hexes?" Effie asked. She was one of the victims, so I hoped she'd be able to tell if Phillip was lying.

"I already told the Protector—I did it as a child," he mumbled, like a kid forced to confess and hoping to shame the council for questioning a sick man.

"How did you pass the oath-taking with that in your history?" Violet Bark asked. "Everything must be examined. Not all mistakes are disqualifying. We might still have allowed you to join the council."

"What about her?" Phillip pointed to me.

A decent way to avoid the question everyone really wanted answered: If the council oath was ineffective, what else had slipped through?

"She shows up, and people start dying. She's as bad as her mother."

I tried to answer, but the restraining spell wouldn't let me speak. It was a masterful piece of spellcraft—clearly something only council members could cast. I tried to reach Destroyer, but all I got was a headache.

Then came a soft series of taps on my window.

He was watching. Maybe I would be rescued by a flock of his bird army.

Mark placed his hand on my shoulder and sent me a calm wave of confidence. He couldn't take sides—not openly—but I felt his support. I needed it.

"Do not try to deflect our questions," Dolph said, his voice swelling with alpha power. "You invited Cossi to Henbane. Are you now suggesting she's your accomplice? She wasn't even thought of when you cast those spells."

45

"We should search this place," Effie said, cutting through the accusations and heading straight for proof. "He must have kept records."

"Why would I do that?" Phillip wheezed. "If I were guilty of these crimes, it would be stupid to keep evidence."

"He's bluffing. There's something here," I said. It didn't matter that I was still a suspect. I was going to help take Phillip down—and deal with the consequences afterward. "I don't need my powers to see how obvious it is."

"Yes," Mark said, giving my shoulder a reassuring squeeze. "He's definitely kept something."

Dolph's alpha power surged through the room. You didn't have to be a shifter to feel like cowering.

"We will find it," he said to Phillip. "Make it easy, and we will show mercy."

Phillip grimaced a smile and stared at me. "I said I would do this." He paused, then turned to glare at Mrs. V.

"As Cossi said, please feel free. It's not going to turn out how you think."

She was encouraging him to expose my coercion power. I wasn't ready for that. And it would shift focus away from Phillip. I opened my mouth to protest—then stopped.

Mrs. V wouldn't put me in that position without reason. I had to trust her.

Phillip tipped his head, addressing the waiting council.

"I tried to protect us by monitoring her, but Cossi Fortuna has a forbidden power. She can force obedience. I'm certain she's used it more than once."

"Do you need help?" Destroyer asked in my mind. The restraining spell must have been weakening. "I feel your fear, but you are at home among strong witches."

"I think I'm fine", I replied.

"Is this true, Patience?" Mr. Macy asked. "Why didn't you tell us?"

"Perhaps she is not the Protector we need anymore," Phillip added, trying to tear everything down with one last grasp.

But it wouldn't work. If I had to be sacrificed for the good of the island, then so be it. I'd only been a witch for less than two months. I could deal.

"This is just a delaying tactic," Mrs. V said. "Test her."

Jeffery stepped behind me and placed a hand on my shoulder. "Center yourself. This won't hurt. Let us in, and we'll close this matter."

Mrs. V nodded. "It will be fine."

"Stop worrying," Destroyer said. "They cannot harm you because I will rain down vengeance."

I imagined every bird on Henbane pooping on the council, and it actually helped. I didn't feel so alone.

The council surrounded me—all except Phillip, of course. Jeffery kept his hands in place while the others formed a circle, touching shoulders. It was a little claustrophobic, and not being able to see Phillip through the ring of bodies made it worse.

"You'll feel me in your mind," Jeffery said gently. "I'll be fast, I promise."

He didn't wait. I felt a warmth flowing through me—not hot, more like sipping cocoa on a snowy day.

"Interesting," Jeffery murmured.

The other council members murmured their agreement, as if afraid to break the calm.

"I'm going to ask you to use this power—twice," Jeffery said. "First, make Phillip tell you a secret important to you, and only you."

That was a challenge. Most of my questions were about why he brought me here—probably important to everyone. Then inspiration hit.

"How did my parents keep in touch with you?" I added the full force of my power, a strong wish to know.

Nausea twisted in my stomach, and Phillip gave a creaky laugh.

"Good," Jeffery said, glancing at him. "Now phrase the same question as if his actions were a threat to Henbane."

I paused for a second. Yes—keeping in touch with someone who made the island visible was a huge threat. I shaped the question in my mind and sent the compulsion again.

Phillip groaned. "No! I won't... I... Because I couldn't risk not knowing their plans. If they decided to return and face their punishment, everyone would know it wasn't her. It was me."

46

I gasped—shocked and suddenly released from the council's control.

"What did you do? How could you send us away?"

"Wait, Cossi," Jeffery said, nodding toward Mrs. V. "I think Patience has been keeping a secret from you."

The council members shifted back, allowing me to see the whole room again. Mrs. V's emotions flowed from her—relief, pride, and joy.

"Your power isn't coercive," she said. "You're a protector. I suspected it, but I needed confirmation. We'll talk about what that means when we're done with this problem."

I pushed down all the questions that erupted at her words. Phillip was more important right now. She walked over to where he was struggling to rise from the stool.

"You broke my memories," Jeffery said, stepping closer. "You hexed people—including me and several of our fellow council members. Cossi broke the hexes, and now the gaps in my head are healing. You cannot continue in any position on this island."

"Make him tell us where the proof is hidden," Dolph

said. "We'll need it—for the rest of the island, and the wider world."

Within minutes, we had Phillip's diary in hand.

Effie flipped it open, scanning a few pages.

"Not even in code. You arrogant ass, Phillip Raziel."

"If we want to keep this quiet until the visitors leave, we can't wait to read through his ramblings," Dolph said. "Cossi, we need him to tell us."

I looked at Phillip—and despite everything, I felt a flicker of pity.

"We should put him to bed," I said. "No matter what he's done, Phillip is very ill."

The council grudgingly agreed. It made me wonder why I'd assumed they were all inherently kind.

Once he was settled, I asked everyone to give us space, then pulled a chair up beside the bed.

"You might as well tell us everything," I said to Phillip. "You know I can make you—but I'm not sure you're strong enough to handle the compulsion."

He started to deny it. I saw the muddy brown of stubbornness gathering around him. But then he sighed and stopped resisting.

"You haven't released all of the hexes. Will I survive that?"

"We can't leave people under a hex," I said. "We'll do what we can to give you the strength to face your punishment. No one here wants you dead."

He didn't believe me. That was fine. I let him think in silence.

Mark brought him a glass of water while we waited.

Eventually, Phillip nodded.

"I cast the hexes to make people forget I was a bully. Not

as a child. My parents convinced me life would be easier if I stopped preying on the weak."

"You didn't want that history to follow you?" I asked, though I already knew the answer.

"I wanted to be on the council," he said. "And I needed control over some witches to help. Your mother should've chosen me, not your father. She needed to be punished. I waited for my moment."

"The woman in the pendant?" I asked. "We found it under Martin."

"I put it there. She rejected me too. I never understood how some women could see who I really was."

"Why did you start killing?" Dolph asked, his alpha magic nudging the truth forward. "And why did you bring Cossi here?"

"People were remembering. I had no choice." He took another sip of water.

I sent a compulsion to answer all of Dolph's question. I tried to keep my disgust from him but I wasn't successful. Phillip sneered at my attempt.

"I didn't plan it. Fate pushed me. I thought I needed to keep an eye on Cossi, but it was her protector power that made her agree. I started controlling Mark to keep the investigation away from me."

I turned to the council. "Do you need to know more?"

"We have enough to prove his crimes," Mrs. V said. "I have two more questions."

"I think the council as a whole is satisfied," Jeffery added. "This isn't the place for those of us he hexed to badger him for details."

"My first question is about Elias," Mrs. V said. "You took his emotions?"

Phillip laughed, but it ended in a coughing fit. He sipped from the water glass again, then caught his breath.

"The fool had no idea. One moment he was full of feelings—love, joy, all the good ones. The next, nothing. You see, I didn't have any left, and it was getting harder to pretend."

I drew back, recoiling as the revulsion in the room pressed against me like a wave of heat.

Mrs. V stepped closer to the bed. "How did you fool us into thinking you'd taken the council oath?"

"Everything the oath requires is tied to emotion," he said. "I didn't have any. So when I swore to protect the island, there was no falsehood to detect. You were all lucky I didn't have bigger plans. Think what I could've done."

"I'm here. Where's the patient?" Doc Rene's tired voice broke the tension from the doorway.

Jeffery stepped forward and quietly brought her up to date on the situation.

"Explains a lot," she said. "A few people came by in the last hour saying their memories were rising and changing. Thought it was the commitment ceremony. Doesn't matter. I tend to the sick, not the pure."

She moved the council members aside with gentle pushes and approached Phillip. I watched as she ran her hands over his body, her magic scanning him like a supernatural MRI. She grunted and stepped away.

"No regret. Interesting." She tucked the blanket around him and patted the pillow beside his cheek. "Did you forget everything about consequences? Or did you just think you were exempt?"

Phillip turned away without answering.

"He will recover," she said. "But his magic is almost gone. I don't know if it will come back." She glanced at him again, scratching her head. "I've heard of people who lack certain emotions—empathy and everything tied to it. I've just never seen a case. I don't know how I missed it."

"Cossi, you can read him better than the rest of us," she said, gesturing at Phillip. "What do you see?"

I closed my eyes—not because I needed to for the magic, but to avoid being distracted by what I'd see in his face. Now that he was too weak to block me, I saw the real Phillip.

"I only see anger, resentment, fear, and hurt," I said. I opened my eyes. "Before I looked, I thought the mist of darkness was just illness clouding him. It's a concealment spell. Something made Phillip kill all the kindness he once felt—for anyone. Even himself."

"And you thought stolen emotions would work?" Doc Rene asked.

"No," Phillip said, grinning once more. "I needed them to fool everyone. And it worked."

Doc Rene shook her head in disgust. "I can't do harm," she said. "No matter what I think of my patient. But I can be disgusted—and that's what I feel for you, Phillip. I hope your punishment fits."

No one had any questions, so we decided to wait until the festival ended. A couple of days to get some perspective sounded great to me. Of course, I still didn't have an alternative place to stay.

"I'll drop by and check on him, feed him, whatever," Effie said. "We'll confine him, Cossi, but I think you're better off staying here than leaving him unattended."

"I have guests to check on," I said—not so much to protest being his jailer, but to remind them I couldn't just sit here.

"It's fine," Jeffery said. "You can come and go. Call Mark if you need a replacement and we'll send someone."

Mrs. V patted my arm. "Everything will be fine. Someone will open the store, and no one will know anything until the council is ready to announce his crimes and the decision on his punishment."

Mark or Lance would come when I needed a break from criminal-sitting. Phillip's health didn't improve, but it didn't get worse either, so I didn't need to give him medical care.

The first day, Mark brought a stack of paperwork and sat at the kitchen table while I said goodbye to guests and cleared the chalets and rooms. I even had a solid stream of bookings starting in two weeks. Zinnia and I had lunch, and she was happy to move into a suite in the main building for her continued work with the committee.

Lance kept the bookstore running as best he could. Phillip's absence didn't slow down orders. I gave him a crash course in the basics and left him to it.

As I headed back upstairs to relieve Mark, I wondered why Phillip had been so thorough in training me. Was he planning to set me up for some book-related crime? I didn't bother trying to puzzle it out. He wouldn't be able to frame me for anything now. The final hexes were gone, and so was his magic.

The best outcome of the festival ending was that the animals came out of hiding. Destroyer set up on a branch of the tree outside the bookstore, and we delved into our witch–familiar relationship. The only thing I avoided talking about was my role as Protector. Not because I didn't want it—but because I was terrified it meant Mrs. V was dying.

The plan bought us two days. I was surprised the secret lasted that long, but with all the goodbyes to visitors, festival cleanup, and the slow return to normal life, no one seemed interested in the case. A spell might've been misdirecting people's curiosity until we were ready for all I knew, but now people were asking about Phillip, not the crimes, but his health.

So here I was, dressed in my most businesslike clothes,

twisting my hair into a bun, and dreading the meeting with Henbane's council.

"I hope I won't be long," I said to Lilibeth, who was on guard duty. "Maybe it's just to let me know what they've decided about Phillip's sentence."

"Don't worry. I've got this," she said. "If they do send him to jail, we can celebrate the end of all the problems tonight."

I didn't let myself hope she was right. The council could've just sent a text for that. Or Mrs. V could have told me. Still, I smiled and said I'd love to celebrate anything at this point.

Destroyer was waiting for me outside the council building. "I am joining you." The way he said it made me feel like I needed protection.

"What is about to happen?"

He flew up and landed on my shoulder. "I made a vow to Tulip that I would not tell. I am the Emperor of the island. I do not break promises. And it is impertinent for the council to expect me to stay away."

At least I'd have some entertainment.

The council was seated in a row. D's dad was in attendance for the first time since I'd been involved. He smiled at me, and I was reminded of a comment D made when we were helping Jeffery—Batiste did look like an aging roadie in a Grateful Dead T-shirt and frayed jeans.

"Cossi, please take a seat," Dolph said. "We have a few items to discuss."

Everyone was shielding their emotions. Mine, on the other hand, were on full alert. Fear. Why are they hiding things? Abandonment? Okay, maybe not... but I definitely feel like an outsider for the first time. Had they decided I was a risk after all?

"Stop fretting, Cossi," Mrs. V said. "Just listen."

I'm not sure telling someone to stop freaking out has ever worked, but I tried.

"It is fine," Destroyer said. "You worry too much."

Jeffery stood and cleared his throat, holding a sheet of paper in his hand.

"Let's start with Phillip Raziel. The council has reviewed all the evidence presented. Our own observations of his behavior when confronted support his guilt. The Protector is convinced he remains a threat to the island, even in his weakened state."

"Whether his magic returns or not," Ashley—the island's accountant—added with an exaggerated eye roll. "We don't need to stand on such ceremony, Jeffery. He's guilty. He deserves the punishment."

"The whole agenda needs to be treated as equally important," Dolph said. "It'll just take longer if you interrupt."

Jeffery glared at them, then continued. "We agree his punishment is to be imprisoned for life. If his powers return, they will be suppressed. He must live as a plain human."

Wow, I thought. That must be the worst punishment they could imagine.

"Good decision," Destroyer said. "Saves me from exacting retribution on the evil one and frees the innocent."

I kept my face neutral. I didn't want to distract the council any more than I already had. "What about Billy and Tony?" I asked. No one had given me permission to speak, but I wasn't under a gag order either.

Jeffery nodded like I'd asked the exact right question. "They will be offered the right to come home. If they choose that option, they must perform cleansing rites. They may also stay in prison—apparently, they enjoy the peace for their research—or request placement in another community."

Fair options. I mean, they'd both killed someone, but it was clear now that Phillip had used them like weapons.

"Phillip will be gone before you return to the bookstore," Dolph said.

48

"Our next item is to offer you the vacant seat on the council, Cossi." Jeffery smiled at me as he made the announcement.

How could I possibly be on the council to guide Henbane? I'd only lived here a short time. I didn't know more than a handful of the residents. I barely understood my powers.

"I can see your doubts," Mrs. V said. "You are the right candidate. But it's entirely up to you. You can take a day or two if you like."

Now I was really worried—she was being kind and patient. I aimed a thought at Destroyer, hoping for advice.

"We will rule the world together," he declared. "I will direct the birds and prey animals. You, the witches and shifters."

I was not getting on his empire-building train. "If you think I'm the right person," I said, "then I accept." I hadn't planned to say that, but the words felt right.

Mrs. V beamed, and despite the shielding spell, I saw the pride glowing from her.

"Excellent. We'll prepare the oaths, and perhaps I can explain what your role will be later."

Dolph glanced at Ashley to make sure she noted it in the minutes.

"You'll be the council representative on the current committee," he said. "We've received multiple requests from members and have agreed to add that to your responsibilities."

Because clearly, the council seat and protector duties weren't enough. I should've seen it coming, given how involved I'd already been.

"The final item on the list for today is regarding the bookstore," Jeffery said, setting his paper on the table and looking straight at me. "We know this is a lot, Cossi. And yes, we've been shielding our emotions. We didn't want our feelings to sway your decisions."

He took a breath. "Our request is that you take on the bookstore. Phillip prepared you for it. We can't guess his motives, but you're the best person to step in."

"I have The Inner Spell," I said. "And whatever the assistant protector role requires—plus council duties and the committee. And I still have so much to learn about my magic... and this whole life. Surely someone else can take over Phillip's business."

It felt like a litany of excuses—but they were real reasons.

"You might feel differently after sleeping on it," Ashley said. "You get the apartment too—no need to stay up at the chalets. We'll do a cleansing ritual, and it's yours."

"You can ease into the council role," Mrs. V added. "And please, don't think of yourself as the assistant Protector. You're not in training."

I guess she was right. I was a Protector. I didn't have a

clue what I was doing, but she was my teacher—not my boss.

"You're overwhelmed," Jeffery said. "Understandably. Take a few days. Get used to island life without a festival... or a murderer. Talk to your friends."

"Yes," Rothtect agreed. "It will take three days to prepare for the swearing-in. I'm sure D and your other friends will have advice."

The shielding lifted completely and a wave of acceptance rolled through me. I hadn't realized how off I'd felt without the usual swirl of emotions around me.

"I'll sleep on it," I said. "No promises."

49

Before I actually slept on it, I joined my friends at Sheena's bar. Being on the edge of the shifter village put just enough distance between me and the main street to lift the weight of all the decisions I still had to make.

"We'll help with everything," Lilibeth said. "I don't know what you need yet, but you're not alone."

Lance called for a third round of beers. "It would be good to have a younger witch on the council," he said while we waited. "Not that I think the basic rules are bad, but a little innovation would be great."

"Like getting you your own business?" Mark asked. "You've been trying for a while to get a plan through the council."

The server placed our beers and a basket of bread on the table. I didn't know if it was the stress of the last few days or something about being a witch, but I was starving. We'd already had burgers and fries—I should have been full— but I still reached for a slice of bread and the honey butter.

"I've given up on that," Lance said. "It takes something I

don't have to be a business owner. I kind of like being the employee."

"It's not that hard," D said. "But I guess if everyone on the island owned a business, there'd be no one left to hire."

I let the evening stay celebratory. I needed to think through the decision to take on a second business—but not tonight.

We wrapped up around midnight and within the hour, I was curled up in bed—wide awake, but snuggled in.

As promised, Phillip was gone.

More than that, all traces of him had been packed up and moved. The place didn't feel empty so much as... ready. Ready for a new life.

I liked my room. If I lived here full time, I could get rid of the old protection spell. Turn the small side room into a real office. Phillip's bedroom would make a great library—if that was necessary, with an entire bookstore downstairs. And I could definitely make the place more crow-friendly.

I wanted to say yes to everything the council had asked —but that meant I'd need help.

Lance's words echoed in my head. Having a manager for both businesses would solve the capacity problem.

I yawned, suddenly tired enough to sleep.

THE NEXT MORNING, I made toast and ordered an espresso machine online.

Then I called Lance and offered him the bookstore to run. He said yes before I even finished the question.

I could find someone else later to manage The Inner Spell. I had time now—we weren't chasing a killer every week.

My decision was made. Henbane was my home. And I wanted to help remove the stain Phillip had left behind.

I sent a text to the entire council: *I accept it all.*

Mrs. V responded first: *Of course you do. Come to the cottage. We have a problem in Vancouver.*

What's the problem in Vancouver? Murder Magic and Mayhem is available now. Cossi is faced with another murder to solve. This time, she is stuck in the middle of a city full of plain humans. Grab your copy now to watch her walk a delicate line.

If you enjoyed reading A Spell To Discover please consider helping other readers to find the story by leaving a review.

FREE BOOK

Claim your copy of Magic Will Out when you sign up for my newsletter and follow Cossi as she seeks answers to her past.

ALSO BY POPPY

For more books by Poppy Bridgeman

scan the QR code below.

ABOUT POPPY BRIDGEMAN

Hi, I'm Poppy Bridgeman, the cozy mystery alter ego of Canadian author P A Wilson. Poppy was "born" because sometimes stories need a gentler touch—with a little magic, a dash of humor, and plenty of sleuthing spirit.

As Poppy, I write the *Witch of Henbane Island* series (where witches and festivals collide with mysteries), the *EB Eats Culinary Mysteries* (a small-town diner, a determined heroine, and murder on the menu), and the *Pages & Paws Bookstore Mysteries* (a Devon bookshop, two mischievous corgis, and plenty of secrets tucked between the shelves).

When I'm not tangled in my characters' escapades, I'm happily tangled in yarn—I knit, weave, and doodle in sketchbooks between writing sessions. I also love to travel, finding inspiration for charming settings, quirky characters, and suspicious strangers wherever I go.

Home base is the Vancouver area, where I juggle writing as both Poppy and P A Wilson. Whichever name is on the cover, I'm always chasing the next story.

ACKNOWLEDGMENTS

People think that the process of writing is solitary. That's not the case for me. I have help from so many people it would be hard to acknowledge everyone, but I'll give it a try.

The support and inspiration I get from my writer's groups is incalculable. The Vancouver Writers Social Group opens my mind to other ways of telling a story. The Royal City Literary Arts Society gives me the opportunity to meet and share with other writers who have more knowledge than I do. The Other 11 Months group is where I learn about getting the words on the page. And my critique group who helps me find the best parts of the story I want to tell. Thanks to all of the members of these great groups.

Last of all, but definitely a huge part of Murder Magic the process, my beta readers. These are the people who love stories and are willing, and more than able, to tell me if my finished story is ready for you, my readers.

www.ingramcontent.com/pod-product-compliance
Lightning Source LLC
Chambersburg PA
CBHW030224180626
46810CB00008B/2957